SAVING SANDCASTLES

LOBSTER BAY BOOK 1

MEREDITH SUMMERS

DESCRIPTION

A breezy feel-good beach read about trust and friendship set in a quaint seaside town on the coast of Maine.

Claire Turner finally has everything she wants. A successful business, a small bungalow near the beach, and the camaraderie of her two best friends. She's successful and independent—something she would never have thought possible before her husband's midlife crisis and their subsequent divorce.

When a rival business opens across the street, Claire worries that she could lose everything she's worked for. Her entire sense of self-worth is tied up in her bakery and café, Sandcastles, and she suddenly finds herself taking desperate measures to make sure she doesn't lose business to the newcomer. Is Claire overreacting? Her friends think it's possible, but will they be able to talk her off the ledge before she does something drastic?

Her friends are dealing with their own problems. Jane's beloved mother, Addie, has dementia, and it's getting worse. Jane has her hands full trying to run the family inn and keep Addie safe. When Addie wanders away from the inn, Jane faces the hardest decision of her life.

And then there's Maxi. On the surface it appears as if she has an idyllic marriage, but does she really? Now that she and James are empty nesters, things aren't the same, and Maxi worries that James may not be interested in staying married. But Maxi has dreams of her own, dreams that she had to set aside while she was caring for her husband and children. Now that she has an empty nest, will she be able to find the courage to turn those dreams into reality?

This is Book 1 in the Lobster Bay series—a heartwarming journey of friendship, love, and loss set in a quaint beach town with a touch of romance in every story. Join the group of friends as they help each other overcome their obstacles and discover that every cloud really does have a silver lining.

CHAPTER ONE

The new store across the street was nothing to worry about, Claire Turner assured herself as she slid the door to her bakery case open, bent down, and peered inside. Her two best friends were due to arrive any minute for their biweekly morning get-together, and she wanted to have their muffins and coffee ready.

Hmm, what to choose? She had a variety of flavors —pistachio, chocolate, lemon poppyseed, orange-cranberry. As her hand hovered over the muffins, her attention wavered, drawn across the street again. Through the curved-glass front of the case, she could see that someone had painted the trim and put craft paper over the windows so no one could see inside. There was no sign announcing what kind of shop it was going to be. How odd. Probably just a beach store or shell shop. Lobster Bay had plenty of those, certainly nothing to concern Claire.

Not that she should be concerned. Her bakery, Sandcastles, was a popular destination for both residents and tourists in the sleepy beachside town. Business was booming. Good thing, too, because she'd put her heart and soul into her place, never mind her life savings. It had all been worth it to reinvent herself after her nasty divorce and prove that she could succeed all on her own.

Claire tore her gaze from the store and quickly chose two muffins then dug out a chocolate croissant for herself and put them all on a tray. The pleasure of eating it would be worth the calories, even though they would probably take up residence immediately on her hips.

"Don't forget some muffins for Jane's mom," Hailey Robinson, Claire's assistant, shot over her shoulder as she squeezed past Claire in the small space behind the case on her way to ring up a box of cupcakes for a customer.

"Thanks!" Claire reached back in, picked the two largest chocolate chip muffins out of the case, and added them to the tray. Claire held the tray overhead as she sidestepped Hailey on her way to the coffee pot and the clean white mugs hanging by their handles from hooks nearby.

Claire didn't know what she would do without Hailey. The single mother was much more than just an assistant. Hailey knew everything about running Sandcastles, and Claire could trust her to fill in when Claire couldn't be there. Claire was grateful that the bakery was successful enough that she could pay Hailey a good living wage.

Claire bagged the chocolate chip muffins, tipped the coffee pot's contents into three mugs, arranged them and the plate on a tray, and left Hailey in charge of the customers while she went outside to meet her friends.

Claire navigated past the sandwich board, which announced her daily specials in brightly colored chalk, to an empty table on the brick sidewalk, where she could see the ocean at the end of the street. The sidewalks were wide, and the section in front of her café, designed for outdoor seating, was separated from the common walkways by tall planters loaded with lush leaves and colorful flowers.

She'd barely set the tray down when she spotted her friends a few stores down. Jane, tall and willowy, was laughing at something Maxi had said. Warmth bloomed in Claire's chest as she watched Jane's unfettered smile. It wasn't often that Jane smiled like that these days.

As Jane walked, she continually tucked strands of her new pixie haircut behind her ear, as if self-conscious about the change. The haircut suited her. The silvery-gray color complemented her fair skin tone, and the cut highlighted her delicate features. It was a big change for Jane, who hadn't done much to her appearance since her husband died more than a decade ago. It was about time Jane started caring about herself again.

"I've got everything ready for you guys." Claire greeted her friends with a hug and herded them to their seats, where their muffins and coffees—fixed the way she knew they liked them—were laid out. Jane fussed with her hair one more time then smoothed her white-and-navy striped tank top over her navy capri pants before sitting and placing a muffin and coffee mug in front of her.

Maxi plopped down in her chair, took a sip, and let out a sigh. "Ahh, caffeine."

Maxi was dressed more casually than usual in a yellow-and-white flowing gypsy skirt and loose white top. Instead of thrusting her hair into a bun or a chignon, a style Claire suspected was encouraged by her husband, her blond hair was loose, the silver-tinged strands curling around her shoulders and tucked beneath the wide brim of a straw hat.

"Is James away?" Claire brushed flour off her apron before sitting down. She wasn't dressed nearly as nicely as her two friends in her usual uniform of frosting-stained apron over her plain gray T-shirt and jeans.

"Yep, conference in Ohio," Maxi said around a mouthful of muffin.

Claire caught Jane's raised-brow look from across the table. Maxi's husband was the president of the Lobster Bay Bank, and Claire and Jane had noticed that Maxi always dressed more casually when he was away. Claire liked James, but she knew that he valued appearances, and *casual* was simply not a word in his repertoire.

"So how's everything going with you guys?" Jane asked.

"Great. I'm getting the house in order now that we have an empty nest." Maxi plastered a smile on her face, but something in her tone told Claire that things might not be that great. Not that Claire would pry. They'd been friends long enough to respect each other's privacy, and she knew Maxi would open up if she wanted to talk.

"Good here," Claire said. Forcing herself *not* to look at the mysterious shop across the street, she took a bite of the chocolate croissant. The dark chocolate filling was decadent enough to soothe her worries about the other shop, not to mention the small water stain she'd spotted in the ceiling of her own. "I've hired Sally to do some repairs."

Like many of the buildings in the village, Sandcastles was quite old. Claire loved the vintage details—the tall tin ceilings, the crown molding, and the wide pine floors. But repairs came along with those. Luckily she ran her business well and had money in the budget for them, a fact of which she was proud.

"She'll do a good job," Jane said. "We've had her do some things at Tides."

"How are things going at Tides?" Jane's family had owned the bed-and-breakfast on the beach for generations. It had been run by her great-grandparents then her grandparents then her parents. Jane's dad had died long ago, and her mother, Addie, had run it on her own until her recent memory problems had surfaced. Jane had to take an early retirement from her accounting position so she could help out. Claire was never sure if she should ask Jane about Addie. She wanted Jane to know she cared, but she didn't want to put a damper on the conversation if Addie was having one of her bad days.

"Things were going smoothly this morning. Mom was like her old self." Jane looked at the watch on her wrist. "Which reminds me, I can't stay too long. I need to get back to give Brenda a break."

"Of course." Maxi looked at Jane with concern. "It's good that your mom was like her old self."

Jane nodded, absently breaking a piece off her muffin. She smiled, but Claire could see the worry in her eyes. "Let's hope it lasts for a while."

A burst of giggling pulled their attention to the street. A group of teenage girls in cover-ups that barely concealed anything stood on the sidewalk, clearly trying to capture the attention of the teenage boys lingering near the beach store on the corner.

"Reminds you of when we were young, doesn't it?" Jane's half smile was wistful.

Maxi rolled her eyes then shoved the rest of the muffin into her mouth, pulled a pencil from her straw bag, and proceeded to sketch onto her napkin. "That was a long time ago."

Claire nibbled the flaky edge of her croissant. Memories of the three of them as teenagers bubbled up. Of course, the town had changed over the decades but not as much as one would think. Most of the quaint old buildings were still there, and though new houses and restaurants had been built somehow over the years, the town had retained its old-fashioned small-town vibe despite it becoming an increasingly popular tourist destination.

Claire, Jane, and Maxi had grown up there. They'd had a lot of fun as teens, especially in the summer, when the town's population would swell with tourists.

"Did we ever flirt like that?" Claire asked.

Jane laughed. "They seem a lot more accomplished at it. Do you remember how awkward it was when we were that age?"

Claire couldn't help but smile. "It wasn't all bumbling. I remember getting some results."

Jane smirked. "I seem to remember you getting some results with one of the tourist boys near the cedar tree on the Marginal Way, Claire."

Claire wrinkled her nose and waved her hand dismissively, avoiding her friend's eye. "That was so long ago. Who could remember one particular boy?"

But Claire *did* remember, in a hazy, dreamlike way. The edges of the memory were misty, from a time when she'd brimmed with energy and innocence. It felt impossibly long ago, but she still recalled the hot summer night, the full moon rising over the ocean, and the boy who had given her one of her first kisses on the mile-long path that weaved along the ocean cliffs and led from Perkins Cove to the beach.

It wasn't like she thought of it often, but sometimes,

the memory came up. Odd. With all the boys that had come after, including her ex-husband, she still thought about that one kiss. She didn't even know who he was. She hadn't seen him or his friends after that night.

"What was his name?" Jane muttered to herself. "Teddy? Gerry?"

"Bobby," Claire answered absently, still halfway trapped in that thirty-five-year-old memory.

"So you *do* remember him." Maxi glanced over slyly from her drawing.

Claire blushed like she was fifteen again instead of turning fifty come the fall. "I don't. Not really. I mean, it was thirty-five years ago. I doubt I'd recognize him if we met on the street."

Brushing her hair out of her narrowed eyes, Maxi looked at Claire like she didn't believe the stammered excuse.

Claire needed a change of topic. She pointed to the napkin Maxi had been working on. "That's a great sketch."

Maxi glanced down and shrugged. "Just a doodle."

But it wasn't *just a doodle*. It showed one of the girls looking up, enraptured, at a boy whose figure was ominously in shadow. The sketch was exquisite and intricately detailed from what Claire could see before Maxi quickly shoved it into her bag.

"I have to get back." Jane looked apologetic.

Claire jumped up, her chair screeching along the bricks as she stood. She turned to face Jane, who started gathering up the trash on the table.

"Wait here a minute. I'll get you some muffins for Addie."

Claire disappeared into the shop. She found the bag she'd set in a corner earlier—not near the back where she suspected the roof leaked—and hurried back out. She passed the bag to Jane as she hugged her. "I know how Addie loves these."

Jane smiled and clutched her tight. "Thank you. I really appreciate it."

Claire beamed. "What are friends for?"

She hugged Maxi as well. As she pulled away, her gaze settled on the store across the street again. The teens had moved on, and now she had an unobstructed view. Her smile faded.

Her friends must have noticed because they both turned their gaze in that direction.

"Oh! I forgot to mention, I know who's moving in over there." Jane's tone held a hint of excitement at knowing a secret.

"Really? Who?" Claire tried to keep the anxiety out of her voice.

"Bradford Breads."

Claire's stomach swooped. She snapped her gaze from the store across the street to Jane. "A bakery?"

"It's not really a bakery," Jane said. "Not like yours. They only sell bread."

Claire glanced back at the store. The papered windows seemed to glare at her menacingly. Where had she heard of Bradford Breads before? Weren't they some sort of chain? Chain stores were always the bane of the small business owner. Better recognition, lower overhead, and therefore, lower prices.

"Claire?" Maxi was staring at her. "Surely you aren't worried about them. They don't sell pastries like you do."

"Yeah," Jane agreed. "I went to one of the stores up in Bar Harbor years ago. They make good bread but no pastries, and certainly no sandcastle cakes. It's a totally different product. Besides, no one can hold a candle to your baked goods."

Her friends were right. She only sold a few types of bread. She was overreacting. She plastered on a smile so her friends wouldn't worry. "You're right of course. It's just a little disturbing that a bakery would move in across the street from another bakery."

Jane shrugged. "Maybe not. Since you don't sell bread, it could be a strategic move. Once the customers get their pastries at Sandcastles, they can pick up fresh-baked bread at Bradfords."

Or skip buying pastries and just get the bread.

Claire pushed the thought away. Now she was being paranoid. "I suppose you're right. Nothing to worry about at all."

The response appeared to put her friends at ease, and they left. But as Claire picked up the tray and made her way back into the bakery, she couldn't suppress that seed of worry that insisted on pushing its way into her thoughts.

❦

"Did Claire seem overly bothered about that bread store, or was it my imagination?" Maxi glanced back over her shoulder at Sandcastles as she and Jane walked down toward the beach, where they would part ways.

Jane grimaced. "Maybe I shouldn't have mentioned it."

"She would have found out anyway. I just hope she doesn't do something drastic. She's probably back at the bakery researching Bradford Breads right now." They turned down Beach Street, and Maxi took a deep breath of sea air. At the end of the street was the ocean with its crashing waves and white sand beach. Jane's inn was a quarter mile down the beach, and she liked to walk back at the edge of the surf. Maxi's house was up on the cliff, and she would walk home on a path called the Marginal Way, which skirted along the very edge of the cliffs. It was all very beautiful and leisurely, but that was part of her problem. Maxi had too much leisure time.

Jane's pace slowed. "What do you think she would do?"

Maxi shrugged. "Who knows? You know Claire: act first and think about the consequences later."

Jane laughed. It was a running joke between the three of them that Claire could be impulsive. The funny part was the Claire didn't always see it that way. Maxi supposed they each had their own quirks, and it was great that they could try to steer each other in the right direction when those quirks took over. Jane liked to play it safe a bit too much, and Maxi supposed she was a little too easy going, too accepting of people's inconsiderate behavior, too ready to sacrifice what she wanted to please everyone—like James, for instance. Troubling thoughts of her marriage caused her to frown.

"Maybe we need to call an evening meeting and feel her out a bit more. You know she wouldn't want to bother us with her worries, and I want to be there to help her if she needs it." Jane's kind words pulled Maxi away from her selfish thoughts.

"Good idea. But I don't think we should make too much of the bread store. Let's just pretend we want to get together after a stressful day or something. If we build the store up too much, that might worry her even more."

"It won't be hard for Claire to believe I need a break after a stressful day. I've had plenty of those lately," Jane said.

Maxi's heart melted with sympathy. She knew Jane was conflicted about what to do with Addie. She'd been trying to give her gentle guidance, but the truth was Maxi had no idea what she would do in Jane's situation. At the age of eighty-one, her mom was as sharp as ever. "I'm sorry you're going through all this. I wish I could do more."

"Thanks, I don't think there's anything anyone can do. I just have to do the best I can. Besides, we all have our troubles."

Maxi looked away from Jane's probing eyes. She wasn't surprised her friend had noticed that something was off. They'd been close for too long for her not to see it, but Maxi wasn't ready to voice her troubles yet. In fact, she wasn't even really sure that she and James had troubles. Maybe they simply needed to adjust to life being the two of them again.

They stopped at the beach, and Jane slipped her sandals off. "Okay, I'll send a text later today."

"Perfect. I'll be looking forward to it."

They said goodbye, and Maxi headed off toward the path.

CHAPTER TWO

Claire tried to focus on baking, but one name kept creeping into her thoughts. *Bradford Breads.* Huffing out an exasperated breath, Claire shoved the latest batch of snickerdoodles into the oven, dug her smart phone out of her pocket, and opened the browser.

Twelve store locations. The new, yet-to-be-announced location would be the "baker's dozen" joked the website. Her jaw tightening painfully. Claire clicked to view the menu.

Breads, breads, and more breads: artisanal breads, multi-grain breads, dinner rolls, sandwich rolls, banana bread, chocolate zucchini bread, vegan and gluten free bread, cheese breads, breadsticks. None of it, not a word as she scrolled through the admittedly delicious-looking professional pictures, made any mention of pastries.

That made her feel better. She looked through the doorway of the kitchen to the café at her bakery cases filled with frosted delicacies. Her eyes came to rest on what she was famous for—her sandcastle cakes. The one-of-a-kind cakes looked like edible sandcastles. Never mind that it took three times as long to make than any other cake. Claire loved hand-cutting the turrets and battlements and pressing the colored sugar crystals to the fondant—a painstaking process. The cakes were popular and set her bakery apart. It was worth the effort. She bet Bradford Breads didn't have anything special like that.

She was making too much of it, just like her friends had said. She just had so much tied up in Sandcastles. Any threat was blown out of proportion. She didn't just sink all her money into it. She'd sunk *herself* into it too.

The clang of metal followed by a muffled curse came from somewhere near the back of the shop. That would be Sally Littlefield, the town handywoman, who was looking into the cause of the water stain that had appeared on the ceiling corner near the coffee station.

Claire's phone chimed in her pocket. She pulled it free, staring uncomprehendingly at the garble of numbers on the screen. *Who would be calling me from...?* She squinted at the screen. *What's that country code?*

Tammi! Her daughter was on a last-fling-before-settling-into-a-real-job overseas trip and had picked up a prepaid phone to use while in Europe. Claire punched the button to answer the call before she missed her chance. Breathless, she held the phone to her ear.

"Hello?"

"Hi, Mom. Are you busy?"

"No," Claire answered at once, even though she should relieve Hailey soon for the end of her shift. Guiltily, she twisted to glance through the opening leading to the front of the store. Hailey's dark hair, which was twisted up into a messy bun at the top of her head, bobbed in and out of view as she smoothly cleaned the front counter and handled the occasional customer. "How's... France?"

"Germany, now. And it's great. We're having the best time!"

Claire listened with only half an ear, positioning herself for more privacy as her daughter recounted the adventures she'd had over the past week with her friends. Although Claire had worried about her daughter in a foreign country, she had to remind herself that Tammi was an adult now, and she had a good head on her shoulders. Plus, she'd convinced her two best friends to accompany her. Safety in numbers. Between them, they knew enough words in local languages to get by.

"That's great." Claire put the mixing bowl and spatulas into the sink.

"Mom?" Tammi asked, almost tentatively. "Is everything all right?"

"Of course," Claire answered, forcing a smile as if a table separated her from her daughter rather than the thousands of miles and ocean between them.

"You know I can tell when you're worried about something, right? What's going on?"

Claire sighed. As much as she didn't want Tammi to worry about her, she couldn't lie. Tammi would know if she did, and she was working on not treating her like a child. "Honestly, it's nothing. There's another bakery moving into Lobster Bay, that's all. I'm a little worried about how much competition it will be, which is silly. They only bake bread."

On the other end of the line, tinny with distance, Tammi laughed. "Why are you worried? If someone else is moving in, out-market them. You've already got a dedicated client base. This other place won't last."

"You make it sound so simple."

"It is, Mom. I was a marketing major in college, remember? I know what I'm talking about. Take a few ads out in the local paper and online. Arrange for a special sale or discount day for seniors or students. Make a few flyers to promote it or maybe some coupons. Everyone will be flocking to your store and ignoring this new place. Trust me."

The idea of people flocking to Sandcastles was appealing. Maybe she should take Tammi's advice and show this Bradford Breads person who the better baker was. But Claire knew nothing about marketing. Then again, she had Tammi for backup.

"I've never really done much to advertise. What do I do?" Claire asked.

"That's a testament to how awesome your place is. But it won't hurt to get more people in. Like I said, it's easy. I would start with some coupons or maybe a special sale. Just take out an ad in the local paper. Maybe put a banner up outside the store."

Claire glanced through the front window. A banner right under the awning certainly would attract a lot of people. Business was good, but more customers were always welcome. And how much could ads cost? She could use some of her savings because surely the leak Sally was working on wouldn't cost *that* much.

"Look, if you want, I can sit down with you after I'm back from my trip. We can hammer this out together."

"Oh, I can figure it out," Claire said, her voice falsely bright. "Easy peasy." The last thing Claire wanted was for Tammi to think she was floundering, because she wasn't. She also didn't want her to think that she was a ditz who couldn't figure out how to run a few ads on her own. Claire might not have done everything right in her life, but the one thing she wanted to show her daughter was that she could be successful on her own merits. If Claire was following her dream and running a successful business, she hoped her daughter would be inspired to do the same.

"Great!" Tammi said. "Okay. Well, I have to go, Mom. Love you!"

"Love you." Claire's answer was automatic and heartfelt.

Marketing. It was such a foreign word, and despite what Tammi had suggested, Claire didn't know where to start or with what money. She had seven thousand dollars in her savings account. Hopefully that would be enough for a few ads with some left for the repairs.

The rattle and muttering from the back had stopped. Claire frowned, wondering if it was safe to approach Sally yet. Cautiously, she moved toward the source of the noise.

"Sally?"

The seventy-year-old woman stepped out of the

back. There was a smudge of grease along one of her cheekbones and a few more on her overalls. The handy-woman with her snowy-white hair braided tightly down her back and her shrewd blue eyes cleaned her hands on a rag. "Ayuh?"

"Have you...?" Claire cringed to ask. "Have you found the source of the leak? Was it an easy fix?"

"Not this time, honey. I'm afraid it's those pipes of yours. Won't last much longer." The creases in Sally's face deepened in sympathy even as she delivered the news in her matter-of-fact way.

Pipes? Claire didn't know anything about plumbing. Faintly, she asked, "How much will it cost for you to fix?"

"Fix?" Sally shook her head. "It's more'n I can do. These pipes are original. You'll need Ralph Marchand to tear out those pipes and put in new ones, if you ask me. He'll know better about cost. But you'd better call him quick. If those pipes go, you're going to have a big mess on your hands."

ane Miller watched a wave rush up the white sand beach to fill the footprint she'd left behind. The ocean breeze ruffled her hair, and she pushed a strand out of her face. The shorter style still felt foreign, but with all her duties at Tides, it was easier than messing with the shoulder-length cut she had most of her adult life.

A sandpiper darted along the foamy edge of the water on long sticklike legs, running forward as the surf went out then retreating just in time to avoid getting its feet wet. Sometimes Jane felt like she was doing the same thing at Tides, rushing forward then back and never making much progress.

Speaking of which, she'd best get back there and make sure things were running smoothly. Reluctantly, she turned and headed up the beach, leaving the soothing sounds of the crashing waves behind.

The wide back porch of Tides, with its row of rocking chairs, was a comforting sight. She'd grown up there, and some of her earliest and fondest memories centered around that house and the expansive beach beyond it. But now, as she stared at the French doors leading inside, the feeling of comfort gave way to anxiety. All the familiar and comfortable feelings tied to the house seemed to be fading away along with her mother's memories.

Even though her mother was still physically in good health, Jane was losing her, but then, Jane knew about loss. First her infant son, then her husband. She had weathered those storms. She would weather this one too.

She laid her hand on the porch railing. The wood needed a fresh coat of paint to survive the summer without being replaced. One more thing for her to worry about. It seemed the hundred-year-old house always needed some kind of maintenance.

The bakery bag crinkled as her hand tightened around it. She used to love walking into Tides and seeing her mother bustling around, tending to guests, but not so much now. Now she was never sure if her mother would be the mother she'd always known or a stranger. She never knew if *she* would be the mother and Addie the child.

The French doors led to a gathering room with faded, overstuffed armchairs, a television mounted on the wall, and magazines scattered across the table. Jane stopped to straighten them, putting everything in its place, avoiding the kitchen, but she couldn't busy herself forever. Steeling herself, she lifted the paper bag full of muffins and continued on. The smell of bacon and eggs filled her nose as she stepped into the warm atmosphere. The kitchen had always been a refuge from the rest of the house, a place where Jane and her sister could sneak treats from the cook, where her grandmother—and in recent years her mother—seemed to spend most of her time. A place for family.

Brenda, about fifteen years Jane's senior, leaned over a pan of sizzling bacon. She had her white-threaded brown hair pulled back into a bun and an apron wrapped along the ample curve of her waist. Every time Jane walked into that room and saw Brenda, she couldn't help but breathe a small sigh of relief. If Brenda was there cooking, then Mom wouldn't be. Brenda had become far more than a cook over the past few years. She no longer went home after the cooking was done. Now she stayed to help care for Addie. And for her part, Jane's mom seemed to recognize Brenda more than she did her own daughter.

Hip to hip with Brenda, Jane's mom—a tall, frail woman nearing eighty who strongly resembled Jane—stood over a large pan of scrambled eggs, mixing them with the spatula. She hummed under her breath, a small smile on her lips, and Jane knew she must still be feeling good. Her mother loved cooking so much that Jane did not want to rob her of that simple joy, but every time Addie stepped close to the stove, Jane feared she would put on a pan or pot and walk away or touch a burner that was hot because she didn't remember it was on.

Smiling, Jane crossed toward her mother. She kissed her on the cheek and held up the bag. "I brought you some chocolate chip muffins."

Her mother's eyes brightened. As she turned away from the stove, Brenda took up the spatula Addie had left in the pan with the ease of long practice. Jane tried not to worry at how seamlessly Brenda took over her mother's post, as if she had done so countless times as Addie's attention waned. Instead, Jane opened the bag and rooted inside until she pulled out one of the chocolate chip muffins Claire had put inside.

With a wide smile, Addie took the muffin and

started gleefully peeling off the wrapper. "Did you stop at Sam's?"

Addie wasn't as lucid as she looked. Jane tried to hide her disappointment as she guided her mother to the long pine table that had been in the kitchen since before Jane was born. Maybe even before *Addie* was born. The table was so old that most of the turquoise paint had been rubbed off. Still, some remained in the cracks and crevices and the turns of the legs. She sat in a chair across from her mom and watched Addie free the muffin from its paper.

Gently, she corrected her mother. "Not from Sam's. Sam's has been closed down for years, Mom. Don't you remember?"

"Oh, yes, of course."

Despite Addie's words, the look in her eye was uncertain. She hadn't remembered, and Jane knew how she beat herself up over forgetting simple little things like that.

In a small voice, she whispered, "I guess I forgot. I'm so stupid, and you're such an angel for putting up with me."

Jane's heart twisted. She reached out and clasped her mother's bony hand. "Not stupid. We all forget things like this now and again." Even if her mother forgot more often than not now.

Jane added, "Claire baked those muffins. You remember Claire, don't you?"

Growing up, Claire had been as much of a constant in the house as Jane and her sister, Andie. Her mom always remembered the past more clearly than the present, even on her lucid days.

"Oh, Claire. Yes, of course I do. Such a sweet girl. How is she?"

Although her mother said all the right words, Jane knew that they were empty. The glassy look on her face and the way that she didn't quite meet Jane's eyes gave it away. She had no idea who Claire was, and that was almost as worrisome as the days when she forgot Jane.

She didn't want to make her mother feel worse, so instead of correcting her further, Jane just told her, "Claire is doing very well. She told me to say hello." Jane stood. She had work to do. "I'm going to take stock of the fridge, if there's nothing else you need?"

Addie's mouth firmed in a stubborn expression. "Of course not. I'm a grown woman. I can do things for myself."

Jane left her mother and the muffins on the table and stepped into the walk-in fridge, leaving the door wide open and basking in the cool air as she checked the shelves. With Brenda staying longer at the inn, they had taken to cooking not only breakfast for the guests but also lunch during weekends. They also baked snacks or left out trays of vegetables or crackers and cheese for the guests to munch on in the gathering room in the afternoon. In Jane's opinion, it had helped them get a higher rating on Yelp, which helped search algorithms. Anything to bring in more customers, something the inn seemed to be lacking as of late.

She supposed it was her own fault. She'd never paid much attention to the running of the inn. Had she really thought that her mother would be able to keep up with it forever? Maybe she'd expected her sister to rush in and take over. Andie had left after high school and barely come back since. Jane should have realized that running the inn would have fallen to her, but instead she had buried her head in the sand and continued down the safe road of her accounting career.

She pulled up a spreadsheet on her smartphone where she kept a running count of everything in the refrigerator. She modified that count and added a few items to the next grocery list. She scanned the shelves one last time, her mind drifting to Claire.

Jane knew Claire, knew her inside and out, just as Claire knew Jane. She'd known ever since Claire had opened the bakery—a sign that she was moving on with her life after an admittedly terrible marriage—that her friend's self-worth was tied up in its success.

Claire led her life with her heart on her sleeve. She didn't respond to logic the way Jane did. Telling Claire that her business would survive because of all its merits didn't help to ease her friend's worry. Claire was stubborn. She would have to see that for herself.

When Jane stepped out of the fridge, Addie was already back at the stove, instructing Brenda as they arranged bacon and eggs into the two covered trays. Jane couldn't help but smile at the familiar scene. Her mother was always meticulous about presenting things to her guests just so.

Noticing Jane's return, Addie cast a quick smile over her shoulder as she hovered at Brenda's side while the other woman carried the tray. "Please thank Claire for that muffin, dear."

She *remembered*. It had been minutes, not hours or days, since Jane had given her the muffin, but there were days when Addie seemed to forget details the moment she heard them.

Jane beamed. "I will."

As Brenda shuffled through the swinging door into the dining room, Addie turned her attention back to food prep, humming under her breath as she took out measuring cups and a bowl. As she sifted flour into the bowl, Jane leaned against the door to the refrigerator and smiled. She counted the cups of flour, noticing that her mother didn't hesitate with the often-used recipe.

Turning, Addie frowned, hands on her hips. "Are you going to help me with these pancakes, or aren't you? I need eggs and milk."

Jane jumped to attention, just like in years long gone. "Yes, ma'am."

As she slipped back into the cool refrigerator, she tried to focus on the fact that this was a good day. She had her mother for however long she was lucid. Sooner or later, she would have to make hard decisions about her care, but until then she would cherish every last moment like this.

CHAPTER FOUR

"**Y**our instincts are as sharp as ever, Sally," Ralph said, descending the ladder he'd used to inspect the pipes at Sandcastles. Despite the compliment, his face was grim as he glanced at Claire.

"Are they bad?" Claire asked.

Ralph nodded in agreement. "Ayuh." He scratched his thinning pate. "I might be able to solder a patch here and there, but I can't guarantee how long they'd hold. They're the original copper pipes, and the fittings break down over time. Could be a year. Could be a day."

Darn it! Claire had known the building was old when she'd bought it. That was part of its charm. But five years ago, the building was in good repair. It'd had no major problems until now, only small odd jobs she'd called Sally to fix. They made things better back when the old building had gone up. Surely those old pipes would hold out for a while. Ralph was probably being overcautious.

Sally gave Claire a sympathetic glance then turned to the town plumber. "Can you fit her in, Ralph?"

"Ayuh." He scratched at his head again, seeming at a loss. "You'll have to close, as I'll need to rip some things apart in here, and it won't do to have customers hanging around. I'll warn you: you'll need to get some repair work to the walls after."

Close in the middle of tourist season? The sunny days were her best revenue days. During the winter months, maybe she could manage to close the shop and not suffer for it, but now, with a new bakery moving in, closing Sandcastles was not an option.

Claire chewed on the inside of her cheek. "How much?"

Ralph rocked back on his heels, considering. "I could do it for about ten grand, give or take. I'd have to price out materials before I can give you a better estimate."

"Ten grand?" The words barely escaped through Claire's tight throat. She didn't have that much in her savings account. And after her conversation with Tammi, she'd relegated a good portion of her savings for advertising. Without it, there would be no savvy marketing. There would be no throngs of customers lined up in front of her bakery to show Bradford Breads who the town's favorite baker was.

"It has to be done," Sally said. Her practical manner helped to ground Claire. She was right, of course. Claire knew she would have to do it, but how would she find ten thousand dollars? Her gaze skated around the kitchen. Sandcastles was her dream. She'd put a lot of sweat and tears into it. She wasn't going to let a few pipe repairs bring her down.

Jaw firm, she said, "I'll try to get a loan from the bank to cover the cost. How long will you need the shop closed?" Two or three days, she might be able to work into the schedule. She could have a grand reopening and use some of Tammi's marketing suggestions to draw in customers. Not to mention, she could continue to bake the custom-ordered cakes at home and deliver them personally. It might work out to her advantage after all.

"About two weeks, I'd say."

Claire took a deep breath. *Two weeks? No way, not right now.* Not with that bakery about to open across the street. The pipes had lasted a hundred years. Surely they could last until the end of summer.

"I'll talk to the bank. I might not be able to swing it

until October." The pipes groaned ominously, as if warning Claire to speed up the timeline.

Ralph raised a brow at Sally then turned to Claire. "Okay, I'll patch the leaks for now. Give me a call as soon as you know when you want me to start."

Hailey noticed the worried look on Claire's face as she let Sally and Ralph out the back. Something was really bothering her boss, and she wanted to find out what it was. It was a slow time of day, so she filled two mugs with coffee and ushered Claire over to a table in the corner.

"Sit. Let's chat. We haven't done that in a while." Hailey pushed Claire into a chair.

"Aren't you supposed to leave now?" Claire wrapped her hands around the mug.

"Yeah, but I have a few minutes. Mrs. Pease doesn't expect me back until four thirty." Mrs. Pease was the babysitter to Hailey's eleven-year-old, Jennifer. Hailey had actually planned to pick up some groceries with the extra time, but she and Claire had become close after working together in the bakery despite their fifteen-year age difference, and she sensed that Claire needed to talk.

Claire was a good boss and a nice person, and she paid fantastic wages, which Hailey was very grateful for. Being a single mother wasn't easy financially, and Hailey knew that most bakery assistants didn't get paid nearly as much as she did. Hailey needed her job, so if Claire was worried, that meant *she* was worried. Besides, she had something important to discuss with Claire, but maybe it wasn't the time.

Hailey cut to the chase. "So, what's going on with the ceiling?"

Claire made a face. "Pipes need replacing."

"Oh. That sounds expensive." Probably not the time to ask for more responsibility and a raise. Never mind that her car was on its last leg and she needed it to take Jennifer to her soccer games and get to work or that she was getting behind on payments toward all the debt her ex-husband had saddled her with. She didn't want to seem ungrateful, and her troubles were not Claire's problem. They weren't anyone's problem except hers, and she would figure out how to solve them.

"It is. But I have some money saved." Claire sipped her coffee, her eyes drifting to the new store across the street. Her face darkened.

Hailey had noticed the store too. She had no idea what was going in there, but apparently it had Claire worried. "Do you know what the new store will be?"

"Bradford Breads."

"Breads? Huh, seems odd to move in across from a bakery."

"That's exactly what I thought." Claire turned her attention back to Hailey. "Oh, but it's nothing to worry about, I'm sure."

Hailey frowned. She got the sense that Claire really was worried and was just telling Hailey that because she didn't want her to worry. "Yeah, sure. I mean we don't even carry bread here, really."

"Right. No competition."

Hailey glanced over at the store. Maybe it sold breads now, but what if this Bradford Breads place decided to expand into pastries later on? Then it would be competition. No wonder Claire was so worried, and on top of that, there was this looming problem with the pipes. She would have to get that fixed, as she couldn't afford a big plumbing catastrophe with a bread store moving in. Plumbers cost a lot of money. Hailey knew that from experience. Definitely not the time to ask for a raise. They would just have to eat more ramen noodles for a while. Good thing Jennifer loved them.

"How's Jennifer?" Claire's question brought a smile to Hailey's face.

"Great. She got an award for summer soccer, and now she wants to play on the Lobster Bay school team in the fall." Hailey's smile faded just a bit. "She's growing up so fast."

"I know how that goes. Seems like Tammi was Jennifer's age just yesterday. Just try to enjoy every minute. Speaking of which—" Claire nodded toward the clock. "You should probably get going."

"Yeah, I suppose. Is there anything I can do to help with the pipes?" Hailey shot a glance over at the new store again.

"Oh, no. Don't you worry about those. Now scoot! I'll go see if Harry and Bert want a refill. It's always slow on Mondays, so I might close early anyway."

Hailey stood, taking her mug with her. She would wash it in the sink on her way out. "Okay, well if you're sure."

"Of course. Nothing for you to worry about. See you tomorrow!"

Claire watched Hailey leave. The last thing she wanted was to worry her assistant. The girl had enough on her plate raising an eleven-year-old all on her own. Hailey had picked up on the fact that something was bothering Claire, so she would have to be careful from now on. But the fact that Hailey depended on her job there was just another worry for Claire. If Bradford Breads stole business, would she still be able to pay Hailey?

Grabbing the coffee pot, she headed over to the corner table where Harry and Bert, her favorite regulars, were chatting away, huddled over a newspaper. The two men were in their late seventies and spent a good deal of time sitting right at that table, reading the paper. From their vantage point, they could see who was coming and going and greet any of their friends entering the coffee shop. They were good customers.

"What's so interesting?" Claire tilted her head to look at the paper.

"That place across the street is finally opening. Gonna have a two-for-one sale on Saturday and a grand opening." Harry pointed to an ad that took up a whole page. A smiling loaf of bread announced the opening of Bradford Breads. Claire resisted the urge to grab a marker and doodle a villain's mustache on the smiling bread face.

"Looks like a big deal," Bert added. "I hope they have rye. You hardly ever find that anywhere."

Claire glanced back at the tiny bread section of her bakery case. She didn't have rye.

"Do you think they'll have some of those fancy breads like oatmeal molasses or honey olive?" Harry was practically salivating.

Claire glared at the new store, picturing all her customers rushing over for fancy breads. "Hard to tell what they'll have."

Her voice came out a little weak, and Harry glanced up at her, his gray brows furrowing in concern. "I'm sure they won't have anything as good as you have here." He glanced back at the case with the lame selection of breads, and Claire's stomach tightened.

"Yeah, whatever this Bradford guy has can't be as good as what you got." Bert squinted down at the ad. "Looks like just bread. Man cannot exist on bread alone. We need pastries, and this is the best place for that."

Claire's chest warmed at the men's loyalty and their attempt to make her feel better, but she knew what they were thinking: the same thing she was. Come Saturday, the whole town would be over at Bradford Breads, and she would be sitting in an empty coffee shop.

"Hey, maybe you should have a sale on Saturday too," Bert suggested.

That might not be a bad idea. Tammi had suggested she have a sale, but Saturday was in less than a week, and Claire didn't have any idea what she would put on sale, let alone know how to take out an ad.

The bell above the door jingled, and Claire turned to greet the new customer. Her cheery greeting froze on her lips when her gaze met the other woman's baby blues: her ex-husband's new trophy wife.

Oh no. She did *not* need this today.

Sandra—or Sandee, as she liked to call herself—looked no older than thirty-five and dressed as if she were twenty despite being in her midforties. She insisted on everyone calling her by her ridiculous nickname. What grown woman chose to spell her name with two Es instead of a Y?

It was probably that fountain of youth Claire's ex-husband had hoped to tap by first leaving Claire for this woman then later marrying her. She was everything Claire was not—blond with a supermodel figure and a defined taste for fashion. And Sandee, petty as she was, never missed an opportunity to subtly flaunt her success as a real estate agent for high-end beach property.

Claire was successful too. Claire had a thriving bakery, *and* she didn't have to lure customers in by trying to look half her age.

"Hello, Sandee. What can I get you?" Claire had to make an effort not to choke on her words, but she was a professional, and Sandee *was* a customer.

"I'm here for your famous cupcakes. My parents are coming down to have dinner with me and Pete tonight, and they loved them the last time they were here. I guess you always were a talent in the kitchen. Not like me. I have far too many other things to do."

Claire bit the inside of her cheek to stop from making a sarcastic comment about how Sandee spent her time.

Sandee didn't seem terribly disappointed when Claire didn't ask what those other things were. She leaned forward as best she could on her pencil-thin heels, showing off her perky breasts through the dress's low-cut neckline. Had she gotten a boob job? Claire didn't want to stare, so she crossed her arms over her own modest chest and waited as Sandee took her time choosing the cupcakes.

"I'll take two of the chocolate, one of the vanilla, and..." Her nose wrinkled. "Don't you have a healthier choice?"

"In a cupcake?" Claire couldn't keep the incredulity from her voice.

Sandee straightened. "A vegan sugar-free option or something."

"You aren't vegan." Unless that was a new development.

"No," she drew out the word, "but it's probably better for you than this sugary stuff." She sighed dramatically. "Better add in another vanilla, then."

Leave it to Sandee to insult the very cupcakes she'd

come in to purchase. Claire pressed her lips tight together and put four cupcakes into a box that fit them perfectly. She sealed it with a sticker that included her Sandcastles logo. When she perched it on the counter in front of the cash register, Sandee eyed the display case, tapping a bright-fuchsia fingernail against her lips.

"Anything else?" Claire tried to keep her distaste for the woman out of her voice.

The blonde shook her head, her straight hair billowing and catching the afternoon sunlight. "No, I don't think I'll buy bread here today. I'd rather wait for the sale at that new bakery coming to town." Sandee turned to look pointedly out the window at the new store, the store Claire was quickly coming to view as her competitor. Sandee turned back, her blue eyes all wide and innocent. "You know they're having a twofer sale? That's a lot. If my folks weren't coming to dinner, I'd spend the money over there. It's like getting double!"

Claire knew Sandee was baiting her, but she couldn't help the thoughts swirling in her brain. How many other people were skimping on buying pastries this week and saving their money for bread?

Even worse, Sandee had a look of triumph in her eyes that told Claire she'd been purposely trying to upset her. She loved that Claire was distressed about the bakery's grand opening. Claire wasn't about to let Sandee get the better of her.

Before she could stop herself, she blurted out, "I'm having an even bigger sale than Bradford Breads on Saturday!"

Sandee lifted a thin eyebrow. "You are?"

"Yes. Huge."

"Better than two-for-one?"

Claire swallowed against the lump in her throat. She couldn't take it back now. "Yes. Buy one, get *two* free."

"You're having a *bread* sale?"

"No." Her gaze dropped to the white box with its pink-and-yellow sticker. "Cupcakes."

"Are you now?" Harry called from the corner. There was real warmth in his voice.

His companion nudged him as they both stood, their chairs scraping back as they prepared to leave. "See? I told you she wouldn't let that bread guy get the better of her. She'll give this new bread place a run for its money!"

Their support gave Claire confidence. Yep, a sale was the perfect solution.

Sandee looked skeptical. She glanced around the shop critically. "You're really going to have a sale? Why don't I see anything about it? Other stores have flyers and posters up whenever they're preparing for a sale."

"I'm going to advertise later," Claire answered, starting to stumble over her tongue. Okay, maybe she'd blurted it all out a bit too spontaneously. How far ahead did one have to plan to get an ad in the paper? How long did it take to make flyers?

"I'm sure you're going to be running a big ad to generate interest." Harry tapped the paper now folded under his arm.

"Oh, sure. There will be an ad and posters, flyers, the whole nine yards." Claire looked Sandee in the eye and forced a smile.

"I hope you're going to offer more variety than chocolate and vanilla. People won't come in for the same old thing."

Unfortunately, Sandee's caustic remark made sense. "Of course there will be other flavors. At least six."

"Oh?" Sandee pursed her lips. "Which flavors?"

Claire's forced smile was starting to hurt. "You'll have to come in on Saturday to see."

"You know we'll be here," Bert called as he and Harry left the shop. "Be sure to save us our usual spot!"

Claire waved to them as they exited into the summer air, leaving her pinned beneath Sandee's narrow-eyed gaze.

"If you're going to have such a popular sale, I can only imagine the enormous number of cupcakes you'll need to bake. Why, they'll have to overflow the display case, or you'll run out! Are you sure you'll be able to bake all those cupcakes in your tiny kitchen in time?"

"Don't worry, I'll manage. I know a little bit about baking. It'll be a piece of cake."

CHAPTER FIVE

laire closed the shop after Bert and Harry left. There were no other customers, and she knew it would be slow for the rest of the day. She needed to retreat to her favorite place—the beach—and think about how she was going to pull off a bake sale.

Her feet had automatically taken her to the river side of the beach, a well-worn route she had walked a thousand times. There the sandbar shape of the beach cut away, and the ocean flowed into an estuary, separating the two sides of beach at high tide. She loved this section of the beach because it was less populated and teeming with creatures in the small tidal pools left beside the rocks when the tide went out. Crabs, snails, starfish, even an occasional sea urchin covered in purple spines.

She stood next to one of those tidal pools, dipping her toe into the water to nudge a reddish-brown crab. The crab—barely the size of her big toe—scuttled backward, raising its front claws at her in warning. It kind of reminded her of Sandee, all bluster but unable to hurt her, though Sandee did it in a more passive-aggressive way.

Maybe she shouldn't have let Sandee's barbs get to her. But she had, and now she had a sale to arrange. It probably wasn't a bad thing anyway. Especially if she wanted to show her customers that Bradford Breads wasn't the only place they could get a good deal.

There was no going back now, and she had so much to think about. Not only did she have to come up with some ads, but she needed to order more ingredients, come up with a schedule for baking, and bring in help. Yes, she still had to think about fixing the pipes, but that was the least of her worries at the moment.

Taking out her phone, she started to make a list. First, she needed an ad in the paper. Preferably one bigger than Bradford Breads. Maybe a two-page ad. It was short notice, but she had worked herself ragged to bake and decorate a sandcastle cake in honor of a retirement party for the chief editor at the Lobster Bay Daily News last month. His replacement, Mona, owed her a favor. If Claire called it in, she could probably insert her ad in the paper in time for tomorrow's edition. But would that be enough?

Claire needed to think outside the box. She needed something that would draw the attention away from her competition, something that Bradford Breads hadn't thought of yet.

She stopped, the ripples of the wet sand hard under her feet as she stood across from the rocky bay, where lobsters were most plentiful. She loved that no one ever came to this part of the beach. The hard sand made it uncomfortable for towels, and the area filled with water when the tide came in, forcing people to move their blankets and gear. As a result, hardly anyone ever bothered to setup in that section.

At the moment, only one other person sat on one of the large rocks on the cliff, the local radio station blaring from their smart phone.

Good idea! She could take out a radio ad. She was sure Bradford Breads hadn't thought of that. She noted it on her phone to-do list. Having lived all her life in Lobster Bay, Claire also knew the staff at the radio station, and she was sure they would mention her cupcake sale on the radio to drive customers her way.

What else? Tammi had mentioned flyers. Claire could get some made up at the copy store and drop them off in a few strategic places. Knowing the other shop members in town did have its advantages, one Bradford likely wouldn't have.

What about the actual cupcakes? How many would she need? And with six flavors—why in the world had she said six? She needed enough of each flavor so she wouldn't run out prematurely.

Not to mention, she had to have an array of her regular baked goods too. After all, a three-for-one sale would allow her to barely break even with the cost of the ingredients, if that. She needed her regular pastries, cakes, muffins, perhaps even a few pies, to make back the money she was spending on those two advertisements. In fact, on Saturday she needed an even larger selection with all the people she hoped to draw in. There was no extra baking time in the day, and it looked like she would be working nights until Saturday.

At least she could start on them right away. Many people didn't realize that cupcakes could be kept fresh for a week if sealed up tight in Tupperware, but she'd tested it out herself, and they came out as fresh as the day they were made. The frosting could be applied the night before. She would need extra hands to help with both. Maybe Hailey would want some extra hours, she could even bring her daughter Jennifer in if she had to. School was out, and two high school students, Ashton and Sarah, had worked in her shop before. She would see if they wanted some extra money to help her out. She would really like to get Jane and Maxi's opinion although they would probably think she was crazy for having the sale.

Just as she was pulling her phone out to send a text to them, one appeared from Jane.

Drinks at Splash 5pm?

Splash, a small restaurant on the beach, was their favorite place to gather for a cocktail. In years past, they'd been able to do it quite regularly. Since Claire had opened Sandcastles and Jane had started helping at Tides, their meetings had been sporadic at best. But when one of them needed someone to talk to, they usually texted a request.

Either Addie must be doing well and Jane had extra time, or she was doing poorly and Jane needed a break. Either way, drinks with her friends was just what Claire needed. She texted back immediately.

CHAPTER SIX

axi left a few minutes early to meet Claire and Jane at Splash. She wanted to walk the Marginal Way to the beach and take her time enjoying the gorgeous view. The sun glinted off the greenish-blue ocean. The foamy tops of the waves crashed on the jagged rocks below. A lone seagull soared above the cliffs.

If Maxi had an easel and her paints, she could have captured the pure white of the gull's wings as the sun hit them and the sea-green hue of the crest of the wave right before it curled over. But she didn't have her easel or her paints. In fact, she no longer owned any. When she was younger, she'd dreamed of making a living as an artist, setting up an easel on the beach, maybe even living a simple existence in a beachside cottage where she could paint the ocean any time of day. But then she'd fallen in love and gotten married, and more practical endeavors had taken over. There was a house to clean and children to raise—none of which she regretted.

Once the kids were older, she might have taken it up, but James frowned on her painting. He considered it too bohemian. She'd given up trying to convince him otherwise years ago. In the end, it wasn't worth the trouble.

Now that the kids were gone, she had plenty of time. James was always busy with work. He'd been spending such long hours at the bank that she doubted he would know what she did with her time. Sometimes she wondered if he even cared. She still kept the house, planned meals, balanced the budget. But she had so much free time, especially compared to her two best friends. Maybe now that James was more established and she wasn't so busy with the house, he would see her desire to draw and paint differently. It had been years since she'd broached the topic. Maybe she should ask again.

As the path spilled out onto the beach road, she took a deep breath. The rich, tangy aroma of fried clams hit her nose. She was lucky to live near the ocean, where there was great seafood. As she passed one of the restaurants, she glanced at someone's plate. Stuffed lobster tail. Her stomach grumbled, hopefully Claire and Jane would want to share some appetizers along with the drinks.

Twinkle lights decorated Splash's patio, already full of people despite the predinner hour. Jane was easy to spot with her silver pixie hair at the corner table she'd chosen on the edge of the deck overlooking the water.

People were still on the beach, though not as many as during the day. A few brave swimmers faced the churning water. Children dashed to and fro, the waves nipping at their heels as they shrieked with laughter and collected seashells. With the sun setting to the west behind them, the sky was painted pink and light blue. Jane turned and waved her over.

"Pretty isn't it?" Jane twirled the stem of the paper umbrella in her drink.

Maxi lifted her hand to flag down a waitress as she spoke to Jane. "Gorgeous. How was your day?"

A tentative smile pulled at Jane's lips. "Pretty good. Mom was her usual argumentative self most of the day."

Maxi gave her a sympathetic smile and plucked at the triangular drink menu perched in the middle of the round table, scanning through the options despite the fact that she'd been there a hundred times before. The waitress came, and Maxi ordered the same thing Jane had—a beach breeze. "Where's Claire?"

"She's coming." Jane traced the rim of her glass. "I keep seeing the look on her face when I told her about Bradford Breads. I just hope she's not getting worked up about it."

"Well, that's why we're here. To make sure she doesn't."

"Might not be that easy. Don't forget, she has her heart and soul tied up in Sandcastles. A bread store across the street might not seem like a big deal to us, but Claire might look at it differently." Jane sipped her drink.

The waitress returned with Maxi's order. After sipping on it—fruity with the smooth taste of rum—Maxi said, "I suppose you're right. Claire has blinders on. She's worked so hard on that bakery. I think it's more than just a store to her. It's a symbol of her independence."

Jane nodded. "And proof that she can make it on her own. Especially since Peter always made her feel like she couldn't do anything except be a housewife."

"We'll just have to help her see the light. The bakery doesn't define her ability to be successful or independent. She's not thinking straight about Bradford Breads. If she thought about it, she might see the possibilities instead. The two businesses might complement each other."

Jane laughed. "You want to help Claire see the light? That will take some doing." Her smile slipped, and her cheeks turned pink as her gaze slid past Maxi's shoulder. Looking guilty, she sat taller in her chair and whispered, "Here she comes."

Maxi lowered her voice. "Maybe now that the news has sunk in, she'll be feeling better."

Jane grimaced. "I don't know. If you ask me, she looks more stressed now than when we left her this morning."

🏵

Claire spotted her friends in the corner of Splash's patio, both nursing pink drinks in margarita glasses. She quickened her step, suddenly excited to tell her friends about her plans.

But first, Jane. Her friend must have called them there for a reason. Jane and Maxi cut off their conversation to wave as Claire stepped closer. She greeted both of her friends with a hug then claimed an open chair at the table. She squeezed Jane's arm.

"How's Addie? Is she doing okay?"

"Yes," Jane answered with a falsely bright chirp. "She had a pretty good day today."

"Really? That's great." Despite Jane's positive words, Claire could see the concern in her friend's eyes. She put her hand on Jane's arm. "We're here for you whenever you need to talk." She wished she could do more for her friend, but talking helped.

Jane nodded and smiled, the tension in her face easing. "I'm fine, really."

I'm having a crazy cupcake sale to draw in customers! Claire wanted to exclaim, but it didn't seem like the time to tell her friends that she'd managed to finagle an ad in tomorrow's newspaper—or the more exciting plans she had to arrange to make the sale come to life. Guilt gnawed at her stomach. Jane had asked for the get-together, and she was there to support her, not to steal the spotlight.

Never one to be the center of attention, Jane turned the conversation to Claire. "How was business at Sandcastles today?"

"Nothing from the usual except Sandee came in just as I was about to close."

Maxi made a face and sipped her drink. "Talk about a terrible way to end your day."

Claire couldn't help but laugh. "Tell me about it. What did you do this afternoon?"

Maxi made a face. "Nothing. It was a boring day, all told."

The waitress stepped up to take Claire's order. Jane and Maxi both ordered another, though Maxi still had half of hers to finish.

Maxi turned to Claire. "Are you feeling any better about the bread store now?"

Since Maxi had asked, Claire figured she could share her plans. "Much better, actually. I have a plan for how to deal with their grand opening sale."

Maxi frowned. "Their sale?"

"This Saturday. They put out an ad in the paper today. One of my regulars told me about it."

"What's the plan?" Jane asked.

"I'm going to have a sale of my own."

"That sounds like a good idea," Jane said with a smile of encouragement.

The waitress had returned and was placing three pink fruity drinks onto the table. "What's this about a sale?"

"A cupcake sale," Claire explained. "At my bakery on Saturday. I'm having a three-for-one sale."

The young woman's face lit up. "All day?"

Claire nodded. "Until I run out. But don't worry, I'm going to be prepared and have plenty of stock on hand in multiple flavors."

"I'll be there."

A man in the corner lifted his hand to hail the waitress. She apologized and bustled over to him.

Maxi was studying her skeptically. "Three-for-one? Why not two-for-one?"

Claire shook her head briskly. The ocean breeze teased a strand in front of her face. She brushed it aside impatiently. "Bradford Breads is having a two-for-one sale. I have to do better if I'm going to attract customers to me instead of them. That means three-for-one. I'm hiring a couple of students temporarily to help me bake them all. I told Sandee I'd be making at least six flavors, and I'll want to have five dozen of each at least."

Maxi choked on a sip of her drink.

Jane cast a sideways glance at Maxi and fiddled with her straw. "That sounds great. If you have a flyer, I'll leave it in the gathering room of the inn to drive customers to the sale, and I'm sure I can carve out some time to help you make them. But, Claire, don't you think you're overreacting a bit?"

Claire blinked. "No. I have to get on top of this."

"Bradford Breads is having a sale on bread. You're selling cupcakes. You don't have to outdo them. They're entirely different things."

"Maybe. But it doesn't hurt to establish myself, and

besides, this isn't just about me. Hailey's worried too. What if my business is impacted and I can't afford to pay her? Jennifer is depending on her, and Hailey is a hard worker and smart. She hasn't gotten a lot of breaks in life, and I would hate to see her without a job," Claire said.

The looks on Jane's and Maxi's faces softened. All three of them had a soft spot for Hailey and Jennifer.

"I understand how you feel," Maxi said. "But maybe six different flavors is putting a lot of pressure on yourself? How will you make them all?"

"I can make them ahead of time, actually. They can be stored in airtight containers, and they won't go stale."

Maxi nodded. "Okay. Sounds like you have a good plan for that. You'll still have all your regular baking, though, so it sounds like you'll need some help. I can pitch in."

Claire's heart warmed. "Thanks, but I don't want to put you out."

Maxi snorted. "Are you kidding? I have nothing to do. It will be fun for me."

Jane reached out to squeeze Claire's arm. "I can help, too, but Saturday is less than a week away. Are you sure this isn't too much?"

"No. Well, it's going to take some work, but Tammi

said I should be advertising and having sales anyway, so I guess this is a good start." Claire slurped down a hefty portion of her drink.

"Well then, if you're sure, we're here to help." Jane raised her glass, and they all clinked.

Claire settled back in her seat, happy for their support, but the look that Maxi and Jane exchanged brought on a load of self-doubt. Had she bitten off more than she could chew? *Was* she overreacting?

Maxi picked up the appetizer menu. "Does anyone want to split some apps? I'm starving."

CHAPTER SEVEN

*C*laire's phone alarm chimed at four o'clock every morning. In the old days, before she owned a bakery and had to rise early to get things setup before she opened at eight o'clock, she had loved to lounge in bed. Of course, that was also before she had Urchin, the fifteen-pound cat that was now sitting on her chest, staring at her with half-slitted, reproachful eyes in an attempt to will her to his food bowl.

Claire felt for the phone, turned off the alarm, and rolled over. Urchin, not to be dissuaded from his task, climbed onto her head and batted at her nose with one paw, claws sheathed.

"Get off," she groaned. "I can't feed you while you're weighing me down."

She pushed the black-and-white cat off, and he

thudded onto the floor then looked up at her expectantly.

"Yes, I'm coming." Claire slid her bare feet onto the thick area rug beside the bed and rolled her neck a few times to get the kinks out before standing up. Urchin trotted ahead into the kitchen.

Claire's cottage was small, but since it was just her, it was perfect. She had everything she needed. Two bedrooms, a kitchen and living room, and a great outside area. Plus, it was only a few blocks from the beach. She couldn't see the ocean, but on a good day, she could smell it. And if she wanted to see it, it was only a short stroll away, or she could take the pink Vespa she'd purchased to cruise around town in the summer.

Urchin insisted on being fed first, so she turned the coffee maker on then filled his bowl. He tucked in without a backward glance, and Claire fixed her coffee. Leaning against the counter, she sipped and watched Urchin eat.

Her mind raced with details of the cupcake sale. Would thirty dozen be enough? Maybe she should make forty. And what about display stands? She should order more of those five-tiered stands she used to display cupcakes when she catered parties.

She finished her coffee, watered the plants, brushed

her teeth, and changed in record time. By the time she was ready to head to the bakery, Urchin had hopped up to the wide window ledge in the kitchen, which always saw the best sunlight in the morning. He was asleep, having forgotten her existence.

Sandcastles was less than a mile away, so she hopped on her Vespa and was there in no time. It was early still, and fingers of sunrise licked at the ocean horizon, casting long shadows down the quiet street. Claire inserted the key to unlock the front door of her shop then peered over her shoulder out of habit as she pulled the glass door shut behind her.

Something was different about the bread store across the street.

Fresh, new letters announced the name of the bakery in the window. The paper had been removed, and she could see inside to the aisles of shelves. At the far end was a counter and a display next to it. A gigantic poster with a golden buttery loaf of bread hung in the window announcing the two-for-one sale for the grand opening on Saturday.

That poster was eye-catching, though. It, like the block letters of the name, was done in bright red. It would draw the eye of everyone who passed up and down the street. On Saturday, there would be a line around the block of shoppers.

Well, fine then. Bradford Breads wasn't the only one who could order a poster.

"You are not going to out-market me." She didn't care if Bradford Breads had more money to take out ads and make gorgeous signs picturing loaves of bread slathered with butter that made even her mouth water. Claire could do one better.

She ducked inside and pulled the door shut.

The sound of a drill made her jump. She'd given Sally a key so she could let herself in early in the morning if she had repairs and didn't want to get underfoot once the bakery was open.

The handywoman stood on a step stool, wearing her usual uniform of worn overalls. Her hair was pulled back into a tight bun, and she had a look of concentration on her face as she placed a screw into the hinge of a cabinet where the door had come loose. When she swung it easily back and forth, testing the movement, it was obvious she had already fixed the hinge.

Claire smiled. "Good morning, Sally. You're here early."

"Ayuh. I figured I'd fix this up and get out of your way before you start the day. I heard about the sale. Lots to do, I'm sure."

"There is, but I've got a handle on it."

"Right, I'm sure you do." Sally climbed down off

the step stool. She removed the screwdriver attachment from the drill and put them both into her old black metal toolbox that sat on the floor, then stood and looked Claire in the eye. "I don't think you need a big sale, though, just because the bread place is having one. Might be better to focus on those pipes. Just sayin'."

"I'll get the pipes fixed. Gotta find out about a loan first. And while I'm waiting, it won't hurt to have a sale." The pipes were important, too, but if Bradford Breads took all her customers, there might not be any point in fixing the pipes. Claire glanced in the direction of the bread store. She could just see the corner of the sign. Was it too early to call Stacy's Signs?

Like many of the residents of Lobster Bay, Stacy also owed Claire. Last year, she'd forgotten to order a cake for her daughter-in-law's baby shower. Claire had filled the order the morning of the shower as a favor, and now it was time to call that favor in. Images of a gigantic sign with a big pink cupcake and the words *three-for-one* in big bold letters near the Sandcastles logo came to mind.

Sally clicked her tongue on the roof of her mouth and crossed her arms over her chest. "I see you've got that look in your eye. But honestly, Claire, that bread place isn't a threat to you. They make savory. You make sweet. You ought to team up, even. It'd be a marriage made in heaven."

Claire jerked her gaze from the phone where she'd been scrolling for Stacy's contact info. "Marriage, my butt." The word stirred feelings in her best left forgotten. That part of her life was behind her. She'd come out ahead and was a better person for it, a more successful person.

Truthfully, she had built herself the perfect life, and she wasn't going to let Bradford Breads ruin it. Nor was she going to "team up" with anyone. If she had learned anything from that ugly time in her past, it was that she could only depend on herself. Depending on another person only brought disappointment.

CHAPTER EIGHT

*R*ob Bradford had always known he would return to Lobster Bay. For most of his life, the town had been a bright and happy memory to look back on when the going got tough. And when he needed a fresh start, this was the place that had jumped into his mind.

Finally feeling the tension of the last few years start to drain from his shoulders, the owner of Bradford Breads leaned back in the leather seat of his five-year-old Chevy Tahoe and admired the newest location of his chain store. He had a dozen across New England, but this location was closest to his heart.

Rob had fond childhood memories of Lobster Bay, where he'd spent several idyllic vacations with his parents as a child before his mom got sick with cancer. Once she'd been diagnosed, there were no more vacations. When she'd finally died after a five-year battle, the family had been so exhausted, no one could find joy in vacations anymore.

Of course, that had been thirty years ago. A lot had happened since then, including his own wife's death five years ago. But Rob didn't want to dwell on the past. This was a new start for him, a fresh beginning that he was looking forward to after all the sadness in his life.

The town had changed a bit since he was a kid. There were more stores, but it was still a small, quaint town. It still had a gorgeous beach, and the town continued to decorate the streets with boxes and beds of flowers in an inviting, charming way. There was also Lobster Bay itself, with the bobbing lobster traps, and Perkins Cove, with its clusters of fishing boats. It was a place where a guy could start a new life.

Movement across the street caught his eye. The bakery. He didn't remember it being there when he was a kid. Someone was putting a sign up out front. He narrowed his eyes and craned his neck forward to see it. A cupcake sale—buy one, get *two* free? He squinted a moment before the date of the sale struck him. He jerked his head toward his own sign. It was the same date of his grand opening.

Was the bakery owner worried about the competition? Rob hoped not. He'd run into this sort of thing before. Whenever he opened one of his stores, the other businesses in town felt intimidated. He hoped the bakery owner didn't feel the same way. He had no intention of putting anyone out of business. In fact, he was very careful about that. With every new location he opened, he made sure not to setup business near another store that sold mainly bread.

Rob loved his bread business. It reminded him of his mom. From the time he could walk, he had grown up watching or helping her knead the dough, peeking under the cloth to check on rising bread, or smelling the fresh scent of it baking. In a way, every time he made bread, he was keeping her memory alive. After he'd graduated from college, he'd stopped buying bread at the store and started the tradition of making it himself. What began as a hobby had grown into a full-time, very lucrative business.

He got out of his SUV, shielding his eyes against the sun to look across the street and through the glass front windows of the bakery. Inside, customers sat at tables. More tables were placed artfully on the brick walkway outside. Planters loaded with flowers and ferns added color and vibrancy to the spot. It looked nice. Cozy. A place he would want to stay and linger. Should he consider something like this for his store? He'd never thought much about the ambiance, but the bakery looked so welcoming. It made him want to step inside.

He should introduce himself to the owner. The information he'd gathered from a representative before he'd leased his location had spoken of sweet baked goods rather than bread. Cupcakes, cookies, muffins, that sort of thing. Without bread to speak of, they weren't in direct competition.

He could make friends and show how their businesses could complement each other. He was starting across the street when a woman appeared at the window. Wisps of auburn hair, which had escaped from being pinned back, framed a pretty oval face. It gave her an air of busyness. Coupled with the apron she had tucked lovingly around the curves of her body, she definitely posed an attractive picture. With her air of confidence and the way she was looking things over as if to make sure everything was perfect—much like Rob did for his stores—he figured she must be the owner.

She monitored the arrangement of the sign in front

of her shop. Then her gaze drifted to him. Her face turned sour, her eyes shooting daggers across the street.

Rob backed up. That must have been the shop owner, and she did not look in the mood to make friends. Maybe today wasn't the best day to introduce himself.

Rob retreated to his store. He had a lot to do before the grand opening on Saturday. He always personally outfitted the new locations with the equipment and supplies needed to open. It was an excuse to make sure it was up to his quality standards. Usually he just spent a day or two and handed the store over to a manager to run it day-to-day, but since he was making Lobster Bay his home, he was going to run the new store himself.

Whenever he'd run into resistance before, he'd always managed to win over the other shop owners. Perhaps before he talked to the bakery owner, he should feel out some of the locals to find out the best way to approach her. In fact, maybe he would start with the bed-and-breakfast he remembered as a teenager. Tides, he thought it was called. He had stayed there once with his mom, and a charming elderly couple had run it.

They might be interested in a standing order of homemade bread to serve to their guests. Next, he could speak with the handywoman listed in the local newspaper who he planned to hire to tie up some odds and ends.

The matter settled, Rob got to work with his shop inspection. Better to find out a little bit more about the bakery owner before he got his head handed to him on a platter.

CHAPTER NINE

*C*laire glared at the man across the street who was stepping into Bradford Breads. Was that the manager? He was about her age, fit, with shoulders that filled out his polo shirt. She couldn't see too many details from across the street except that he had a strong jaw and short-cropped dark hair with shades of silver. If he hadn't been working for the enemy, she might have thought him attractive. *Might* have.

Naturally, he was working for the enemy because he was heading for the bread store, which wasn't open to customers. Only someone who worked there would be able to get in. She'd never seen him in town before, so he wasn't local. And the owner of a franchise like Bradford Breads never did the grunt work himself. He sent lackeys. Middle-aged, attractive lackeys with silver at their temples.

"Is that the owner of Bradford Breads?"

Claire jumped at Sally's voice. "Probably some lackey."

Sally pressed her lips together as she stared unabashedly at the shop across the street. "Could be. I heard the owner inspects all his stores before they open personally."

"That's not him. Look at what he's driving."

Yes, the SUV was an expensive model, but it was several years old. And it appeared to be in good condition, no broken taillights or cracked wind shield. But there was dust caked on the car as if the owner had gone off-roading.

Sally squinted. "Ayuh. I heard those bread stores of his are successful. He probably drives something flashier."

Claire pictured a red Corvette, a short, balding man slipping from the driver's side as his blond trophy wife tottered to her feet on high heels that would get stuck in the sidewalk cracks. Her name would probably end in two Es.

The customer who had been standing at the cash register cleared her throat.

As Claire cashed her out, her phone chimed with an

incoming text message. She ignored it until she'd boxed up her customer's choices and delivered them to her. Only then did Claire fish the phone out of her pocket.

She smiled in relief as she peered at the text. It was the last of her teenage hires promising to come in to bake cupcakes on Wednesday, Thursday, and Friday evening. With their help and her supervision, she would be on top of the last-minute cupcake sale four days away. The morning was going well. She'd already secured an ad with the local radio station, ordered flyers from Stacy, and now had helpers for the baking. She breathed a little easier.

At least until she looked up from the phone to find Sally standing in front of her.

"Good news?" asked the old woman.

Claire nodded.

The handywoman grunted. "Well, that's good because you're not going to like what I found in the kitchen."

Claire sighed and followed the older woman to the site of the concern. What would she find? Rats? A busted pipe already turning her kitchen into the town swimming pool? The floor was dry.

Claire followed Sally to the bathroom, where the handywoman pointed under the vanity. "Got a leak."

Shoot! The pipes. "Can you patch it until I get money for the pipe repairs?"

Sally's eyes narrowed. She rubbed her chin and bent over to inspect the pipes again. "I guess so. But these are old, too, like the rest of the building." She peered back up at Claire, awaiting the final decision.

The cupcake sale was already in motion. She hadn't talked to the bank about the loan for the pipe repairs. She only needed four more days to make it through the grand opening, then she would get the ball rolling for the whole repair job.

"A patch job will have to do. Let's hope it holds until after the big cupcake sale."

Hailey parked the old beat-up Dodge she'd borrowed from her grandfather in the town lot a few stores down from Sandcastles. She turned off the ignition and patted the dashboard. "Now you be nice and startup when I get off work."

Ignoring the rusty groan of the car door, she hurried down the street to Sandcastles. Across the street, something was different. The store now had the paper off the windows and a big sign for a sale. *Oh no!* Would that take business away?

She let herself in the bakery's side door, almost forgetting to pull it tight. The door was another thing at Sandcastles that needed to be fixed. If they didn't make sure it latched, it would swing back open. The last thing they needed was a bakery full of flies.

"Did you see the big sale sign across the street?" she asked Claire as she cinched the strings around her waist.

Claire turned from where she'd been talking to Sally in the hallway. It seemed like Sally had been there more often than not lately, which added another layer of worry. Were there more and more things that needed to be fixed? *Poor Claire.* Hailey knew that Claire wasn't exactly rolling in money. Even if Hailey took some responsibility from Claire's shoulders, she wasn't sure Claire would have extra money to give her a small raise.

"Yes, but we're going to do them one better," Claire said.

"We are?"

"Yes. We're having a two-for-one cupcakes sale on Saturday."

Hailey turned to survey the kitchen with its one oven and limited counter space, already calculating what they would need to pull that off in her head. "How many extra cupcakes?"

"About thirty dozen."

Hailey let out a low whistle. "Okay, we'll have to bake at night unless we're going to have less of the regular items."

"I know. I want to keep our regular schedule during the day but figured we could bake extra at night. The cupcakes will keep, and I'll ask Jane and Maxi to help frost them all on the last night. I've hired Ashton and Sarah to help with the baking, and if you have time at night, I'll pay you extra."

Hailey frowned. A few nights of extra pay wouldn't solve all her problems. Every little bit helped, though. "I might be able to do some extra hours." *If Gramp's car holds out.*

"Great! You can bring Jennifer."

"Shoot! Jennifer has summer soccer every night this week. Maybe I can get Mrs. Pease to take her."

Claire's eyes filled with motherly concern. "You don't want to miss a game, do you? It won't be but the blink of an eye, and she'll be off on her own. Don't feel like you have to come. There will be plenty of hands to bake the cupcakes."

"We'll see." Hailey didn't want to voice her worries or the fact that she could use extra money, so she changed the subject. "What's going on in the bathroom?"

Claire glanced into the bathroom, where Sally could be heard clanging a wrench against the pipes, and plastered a smile on her face, one that didn't reach her eyes and worried Hailey. "Oh, just a little leak. Sally will take care of it." Claire gestured toward the kitchen. "I've got cinnamon rolls in the oven. Can you mix up some brownies?"

"I'm on it." Hailey headed toward the cabinet and pulled out cocoa, flour, and baking soda. "Do you have a game plan? Like how many per night and a list of ingredients, that sort of thing." She put the dry ingredients on the counter and headed to the fridge for eggs, milk, and butter.

"I'm making a list of ingredients, but a solid plan might be good. Maybe I should see if Maxi and Jane want to help me work it out. Jane is so good with that sort of thing. Would you come too?"

Hailey was honored to be included. She loved Claire's friends, who liked to mother her and Jennifer. It was welcome attention since Hailey's own mother had died when she was twelve. She liked to spend time with them, but even better, the invitation signaled that Claire trusted her as more than just hired help. "I'd love to."

CHAPTER TEN

ides was the same as Rob remembered from when he had stayed there as a kid. Even the interior—with the large old-fashioned floral-wallpaper foyer that served as a lobby, the well-kept balustrade of the staircase leading to the second floor, and the walls hung with paintings of the beach and other nearby landmarks—hadn't changed.

At the tinkle of the bells attached to the door, an old woman bustled out from a room deeper in the old Victorian house. She was robust, if thin, her face craggy with wrinkles, and her long white hair pulled back from her face. Although the bell had called her, her eyes were glassy, as if she couldn't seem to remember why she had stepped through the door. She peered around, the wrinkles in her face softening with confusion as she searched.

"Are you looking for Dad?" Her voice was soft, almost girlish.

Immediately, the lost look in her face and the timidity of her voice clicked into a slot in his mind. The woman must have some sort of dementia. Rob recognized the signs, having lived with that very expression for far too many years of his life. Caroline, his late wife, had been diagnosed with early-onset Alzheimer's. It was a disease that not only sapped the memory but also the personality, and finally the very life from her.

He was flooded with compassion for the woman in front of him. What was this woman doing there, unaccompanied? Was she a guest? Rob glanced at the open door, knowing full well a person with dementia could wander off and get lost. He knew just how to handle someone with memory loss.

Tucking his hands into his pockets, he smiled and strolled forward. "Hello. I hoped to speak with the owner of this inn. Would that be you?" he teased.

She giggled. "Oh, Charlie, you know it will be some day. Do you have a delivery? You can bring it to the back with me."

She fluttered her eyelashes at him. He didn't have the heart to tell her that he wasn't Charlie. Not to mention, given how young she seemed to think she was, he would be far too old for her to be flirting with him. She acted like a teenager.

He cracked a smile and shrugged his shoulders, careful not to encourage her but also not to confuse her by correcting her. Sometimes it was kinder just to play along. "No delivery today. But I hope I'll be back soon with the delivery. Who should I talk to about that?"

A younger, harried-looking woman, who resembled the old woman to such an extent that they must be related, stepped out from another archway.

"You can talk to me." Shyly, she tucked a strand of silver hair behind her ear. She was soft-spoken, not like the brusque business owners or overly friendly extroverts he usually dealt with. It was refreshing. Maybe she was someone he could do business with on friendly, trusting terms.

He gave the older woman another smile because that felt far safer. "I hope you don't think I'll be ignoring you, but I do want to talk to this fine woman about potential future deliveries. I have a business proposition."

The younger woman nodded briskly and stepped up, offering her hand. "It's fine. I'm Jane Miller, and this is my mother, Adelaide."

Rob shook hands with Jane. "Nice to meet you

both. I'm Rob Bradford from Bradford Breads. I just opened a store in town. Is there a place we can sit down and talk?"

Abruptly, the old woman sharpened. The fog of confusion left her face, and her voice gained strength. "If you're talking business, then you'll talk to me. I still run this place, you know."

Rob was speechless at how quickly she seemed to shake off the confusion.

Then she added, "At least while Daddy is away."

Lines spiderwebbed around Jane's eyes, her smile turning forced. "Of course, Mom. Why don't you show him to the kitchen?"

The old woman nodded and turned on her heel, bustling away with vigor that belied her age. As Rob indicated that Jane should follow first and he would trail behind, she lowered her voice and whispered, "It's very kind of you to include her. Most people get uncomfortable around her when she's like this."

His smile faded, but he tried to hide it. "I have some experience with dementia." Before she asked more—he didn't want to open that can of worms with a stranger—he lengthened his stride. Not to mention, most people didn't care to hear about a woman in her forties developing Alzheimer's.

Thankfully, Jane simply nodded, a look of

sympathy flashing through her eyes, before continuing to the kitchen.

The room had the atmosphere of antique nostalgia mixed with modern gadgets. Adelaide had already seated herself at a long pine table that had a plate of muffins in the middle.

Jane took her cues from her mother and offered some coffee. Rob accepted, hoping to foster a friendly arrangement between them. While she fixed three cups, he made idle conversation with Addie about the history of the bed-and-breakfast. She remembered a lot about the past, talking about raising children in the same breath as running wild up and down the halls as a child herself. Rob listened to her intently, even when she repeated herself. He always had the time to be kind.

Before long, Jane doled out several cups of coffee and took the seat next to her mother. "So, what did you want to talk about? I've seen your store in town."

Rob couldn't tell by her tone if she approved of the store or not. "We bake fresh bread every day, and in many of the towns surrounding our locations, I like to make connections with local businesses. Bed-and-breakfasts often serve our products for their guests. I thought you might also like to serve fresh bread to your customers."

Adelaide, who had started picking apart a chocolate

chip muffin, nodded emphatically. "That's a wonderful idea! You know, we pride ourselves in having a great breakfast here at Tides, but we don't make our own bread, do we, Jane? What do you think?"

Despite her mother's enthusiasm for the topic, Jane didn't seem as convinced. "It's not a bad idea."

He took a sip of his coffee. When she didn't continue, he raised one eyebrow, and said, "I sense a 'but' in that sentence."

She grimaced. Turning in her seat, she murmured, "Mom, I don't think Claire would like it very much if we started a business relationship with Bradford Breads."

Addie's forehead creased. "Claire? Who's Claire?"

Frustration crossed Jane's face for a second. Rob remembered that feeling. But then she shut her eyes, took a deep breath, and said very patiently, "Claire made that muffin, Mom. You remember, don't you?"

Addie nodded, but it was that blank, empty nod that meant she didn't truly understand. Rob recognized it well.

With a small sigh, Jane turned back to Rob and explained, "One of my best friends owns the bakery in town. To tell the truth, she's a little put out by you moving in across the street."

He'd judged as much by the stony look she gave

him when he saw her across the street earlier. He sighed, pushing his mug a bit farther from him in preparation to leave. "I was afraid of that."

But Jane didn't seem ready to kick him out the door. She frowned, her eyebrows knitting together. "Afraid of it? Why do you say that?"

At least she wasn't ready to leap into battle for her friend and kick him out. He settled back in his chair. His eyes caught on the tray of muffins, and Jane pushed them toward him, indicating for him to help himself to one. Maybe it would help his case to compliment the baker when they inevitably met. He took one, and Jane grabbed a plate from a sideboard and slid it in front of him.

Before he bit into it, he explained, "I'm not here to put people out of business. In fact, I always make sure when I move into a town that there isn't currently a bakery specializing in bread. But even so, it always seems to happen that somebody is put out by my presence. I'm not a threat to your friend's bakery, I promise."

As he met her gaze, he saw something in her eyes. Conflict. Loyalty. Even if he couldn't get a standing order of bread from Tides, Jane might be able to help him smooth out the bumps in his business plan.

He leaned over the table. "Maybe you could help me out."

She seemed surprised, her blue eyes widening. "Me? I don't know…"

"Not with the bread order, though I do hope you'll change your mind. But if you're best friends with the owner of the other bakery in town, you undoubtedly have some influence over her. I noticed the sign for her cupcake sale. I also noticed that it was a three-for-one and on the same day as mine."

When he raised one eyebrow, Jane nodded. "She wants to establish a presence that day."

Rob thought as much. "I would like to set things straight with your friend before this competition gets out of hand. I'm not here to hurt her. In fact, things would go a lot smoother if we could work together. What do you say, Jane? Will you help me?"

❀

Jane nibbled on her lower lip. She should probably just tell Rob she wasn't interested and send him on his way. But the thing was, she didn't think he was a bad guy. Especially not with the way he'd treated her mother. Not once had he tried to avoid Addie or ignore her. Despite the way she butted into the conversation or entertained him with fragments of stories that only halfway made sense, Rob didn't seem to mind. He treated her as kindly as he would his own mother. Jane appreciated that kindness more than she could express.

But if she took him up on his offer—either to approach Claire or to enter into a business arrangement with Bradford Breads, how would Claire feel? Claire had been Jane's best friend since they were in elementary school. The last thing she wanted to do was create friction or add more stress when Claire seemed worried as it was. Even if Claire was being unreasonable.

Claire would come to her senses sooner or later. Maybe Jane could help her along.

Hesitantly, Jane asked, "You mentioned working together. In what way?"

Rob leaned back in his chair, chewing on a bite of the muffin as he thought. From the moment he had stepped into Tides, he'd had an easy, confident way of holding himself, a self-assurance that didn't border on arrogance. He wasn't one of those smooth businessmen who lied to get what they wanted. Jane knew it in her gut.

He swallowed and answered, "We don't have to compete for customers. There's room for them to visit both of us. All three of us, in fact. We could put on promotions together to get more people coming to

Lobster Bay in the off-season. I know I'm doing my grand opening in the summer, but I did enough research to know that while this is the prime time for tourists, people do visit here year-round."

Jane nodded. "You're right. We get a few vacationers around Christmas but nothing compared to summertime. Promotions don't sound like a bad idea."

Rob's eyes brightened, making him look even more handsome. Clearly, Claire hadn't yet met the guy, or she wouldn't be quite so prickly about him moving in across the street. Not that Rob held a candle to Jane's late husband. She swallowed against the lump in her throat that grew smaller each year but never seemed to leave.

"You truly don't mean to put the bakery out of business?"

Rob shook his head. "That would be bad for my business too. I definitely can't make muffins like these. And the locals no doubt expect them. I wouldn't be able to meet that expectation."

One corner of Jane's mouth hitched up in a smirk. She tried to swallow it but must not have been successful because he leaned forward eagerly, encouraged that he'd won her over even just a bit.

"So you'll talk to your friend for me? Help her see that I'm not a threat to her?"

Jane pressed her lips together, but she nodded. "I'll try. You have to understand, that bakery is like Claire's baby. She's put her heart and soul into it. She's very overprotective."

He chuckled. "That I can understand completely. Truth be told, I feel the same about my business."

Jane drummed her fingernails against her coffee mug. "I'll try to get her to soften up, but that's it. I can't in good conscience enter into an agreement with Bradford Breads at this time."

Addie started to protest, but Rob held up his hands in surrender. "I understand. It's not worth harming a friendship." He swallowed down the last of his coffee, scraped back his chair, and took his plate to the sink. "Maybe once the tension has blown over, we can revisit the idea."

Jane stood to shake his hand. "Absolutely."

Despite the fact that Addie hadn't yet stood, Rob made a show of shaking her hand too. "It was so lovely to spend an hour with you. I hope we meet again soon."

"Do you need me to show you to the door?"

He shook his head. "I can remember the way. Thank you—and you know where to find me if you change your mind."

As he left, the kitchen door shutting behind him, Jane couldn't help but notice the glow on her mother's face. It was nice to see her mother happy. So many people talked down to her these days. Rob's kindness had done her good.

When Jane saw Claire again, she could safely say that his business meant hers no harm. Claire had texted her earlier that day about meeting at her cottage that night since her time was limited between now and the sale on Saturday. Maybe if Jane could get Claire to see what she had just learned of Rob Bradford, Claire would rest a little easier too.

But before she met with her friend, she had work to do at Tides. As she started to gather the cups to wash them, her mother giggled like a schoolgirl. She caught Jane by the arm, her eyes aglow. "How nice for him to come here and ask me to the dance. Won't Sadie Thompson be jealous when she sees me walking in with that hunk on my arm?"

CHAPTER ELEVEN

The sea breeze gusted through the open windows of Maxi's house. Waves crashed on the rocks below the cliff on which her house perched at the end of the lane. Maxi, accustomed to the white noise, almost thought of it like a companion. Right then, it was her only companion in the house.

For years, the house had been filled with sounds, shouts, teasing and laughter from her three children. But now, all three of them were grown, the youngest two in college and the oldest married with a place of his own. They were all doing well, and that made her happy, but now she needed more to fill her life, especially with James gone so often.

Maybe a decorating project? Decorating had been an artistic outlet for her over the years. She'd been told more than once that their house looked like it could be in a magazine. And at least that was something that James, too, was proud of. He loved entertaining his bank colleagues there and boasting about his wife's talent.

But the main floor had been redone recently for the kids' college graduation parties. Maybe the bedroom? Maxi climbed the staircase lined with family photos to the master bedroom. Done in cobalt blue and yellow, it had a serene feel to it. Was the color scheme dated? Maybe a new comforter in bright white and some accent pillows would give it a fresh look for summer.

At the foot of the bed, the pillows piled on a cedar chest provided cushioning to use it as a seat. She could get a new cushion for the seat part, maybe paint the wood white. Of course, she should probably clean it out first.

Something tugged at her to open it. Inside were memories: photo albums of her parents and grandparents, locks of hair from the kids, school pictures, and her art supplies that she hadn't touched in decades. Maybe she should just take a little peek at them and see what condition they were in. As she started taking the pillows off the chest, her phone rang. *James!*

"Hi, honey," she answered.

"Sweetie! How are you?" James's voice sounded like he was genuinely happy to talk to her.

"Great. How about you? How is the conference going?"

"Well, you know how they are, just a bunch of boring lunches and sleep-inducing presentations. What have you been up to?"

"Me? Not much." Maxi told him about the new bread store and Claire's plan for a sale. "I'm going to help her out. I don't have much to do with the kids gone now."

There was silence on the other end, and for a minute, Maxi thought James might forbid her to help Claire, but instead he said, "You don't? I guess maybe it will be good for you to help her out for the sale."

He put an emphasis on *for the sale*, but Maxi was encouraged anyway, so she plowed ahead. "I was thinking maybe I should take up drawing again. You know I used to enjoy it so much before the kids, and now with extra time…"

Muffled sounds came from the phone, as if James had covered it with his hand. Then she heard him faintly say, "Be there in a minute," before his voice returned in full. "Taking up drawing sounds like a great idea. That should keep you busy."

Maxi practically bubbled with excitement. "Yes, it certainly will."

"Good, then go for it. I have to run. Love you!"

"Love you too!"

James hung up, and Maxi tossed the pillow off the chest with a burst of energy. *That was so easy!* She *had* been making too much of James' reluctance to let her draw. Had that all been in her mind, an internal excuse because she was too busy with other things? It didn't matter now, she thought as she opened the cedar chest and looked inside, half-expecting the contents to have evaporated in the years since she'd tucked them away. But there they were, row on row, packed neatly. Her old sketchbooks from high school and the scant years after right up to the half-filled one she'd tucked away with the others some months after she'd gotten married.

Her hand trembled as she fished that one out of the neat row. She opened it to sketches in various stages of completion. And then a blank page. Untouched. In the corner of the cedar chest was the box in which she had stuffed her charcoal pencils. The cardboard crinkled as she opened the box and pulled out her favorite pencil, worn almost to a nub. The tip was blunt. A small pencil sharpener was crammed into the corner of the box along with a kneading eraser.

The blank page sang to her. She was reaching for

the pencil and sharpener when her phone chimed with a text.

It was Claire, asking to get together that night at her place to help her plan the cupcake sale.

Of course, Maxi would accept. She could draw anytime, but if Claire needed her help, that was a priority. She texted back.

I'll bring my lobster dip. See you later!

She set the pencil and sharpener back in their place, piled everything else back into the cedar chest, then shut the lid. She placed the pillows on top of it neatly and stepped away, already planning what her first drawing would be.

Right then she had something more important. If she was going to make her famous lobster dip, she would need to head to the store for ingredients. Maybe while she was at it, she would get ingredients for her equally famous chocolate raspberry cheesecake.

The day was looking up.

CHAPTER TWELVE

Claire loved entertaining on her back patio in the summer. The patio had been one of her renovation splurges when she'd bought the small cottage, and Maxi had helped her design it. It was done in antique brick, laid out in a herringbone pattern. It was private, enclosed by a pleasant wood fence painted the same grayish blue as the cottage. Twinkle lights were twined around the top of the fence, and flowerpots bursting with colorful petunias and impatiens hung from hooks spaced evenly all around it.

The area was large. On the far end, she had comfortable wicker furniture, a patio umbrella to shade from the sun, and a gas fire pit. A gas grill and glass table and chairs sat closer to the cottage near the sliding door that led to the dining room. She'd already arranged napkins, plates, silverware, glasses, and a bottle of wine in an ice bucket on the table.

Maxi arrived first, loaded with her signature lobster dip, a box of sea salt crackers, a cheesecake, and a special lobster treat for Urchin. Claire tried not to be jealous at the way the cat cozied up to Maxi. Even after her friend had given him the treat, the cat continued to purr and rub against her legs. The only time he ever wanted to cuddle with Claire was when it was freezing cold and he wanted the heat. But then, Maxi did seem to have a way with pets.

Jane arrived a few minutes later with her platter of vegetables and dip, and Hailey not long after that with a plate of homemade brownies.

"I brought a little gift for Jennifer." Maxi held up a small bag. Jennifer didn't have a grandmother, and the three of them tried to make up for that with occasional gifts.

"You don't have to do that. She'll get spoiled." Hailey peered into the bag. "A sketchbook and pencils. She'll love that."

Maxi shrugged it off. "Just a little something."

"Thank you. Speaking of Jennifer, I have to pick her up in a half hour. Mrs. Pease dropped her off at the soccer game, but I don't want to miss too much of it."

"Then I say we get started." Claire gestured to the

glass-topped table where she'd arranged the food, and they all sat.

Jane produced a tablet and scrolled to a display with columns. "I made you a spreadsheet for ingredients. You'll need to change things for the right amounts per cupcake, of course, and make sure I have every ingredient listed, but the important part is that it's a spreadsheet, so it will calculate what you need to order."

"Really?" Claire watched as Jane changed some figures and the spreadsheet recalculated. "That's much better than my handwritten jumble." Claire pulled a piece of paper out of her pocket.

Jane rolled her eyes good-naturedly. "Everything is electronic now, Claire." She reached for the paper. "I'll just plug what you have here into the formula, and you can double-check. Have you put in an order yet?"

"Just for the flour. I use a special brand, and it has to be ordered a day in advance, so I should get a delivery tomorrow, just in time for baking."

"And the baking schedule?" Hailey dipped a miniature carrot into creamy ranch dip. "We don't have much down time during the day, and there are only a few days until the sale, so I think it makes sense to settle on a set amount of cupcakes that need to get baked every night."

"Good thinking. I've lined up Ashton and Sarah for

the next two nights, and if we bake fifteen dozen each night, we should be good," Claire said.

Jane glanced up from the tablet, looking over her readers at Claire. "You might want to add an extra dozen or so just in case."

"I'm going to see if we can fit some extra baking in during the day." Claire looked at Hailey. "Maybe in the afternoon, when it's not so busy, we could get a dozen in each day. Just in case we fall short at night for some reason."

Hailey munched on her carrot. "Sounds like a plan."

"And don't forget Maxi and I can help," Jane said.

"And me," Hailey added.

"Thanks. I think Ashton and Sarah will be enough for the baking. That's fairly easy, and I'll be there to make sure the batter is mixed properly. Then it's just watching the timer to make sure they don't burn. We only have the one oven, so I couldn't really utilize more than two other people, anyway," Claire said. "What I could really use you guys for is frosting them."

Hailey nodded. "Frosting takes patience and a bit of skill. Patience isn't something that Ashton and Sarah are known for."

Claire laughed. "Yeah. They're good kids but tend to rush."

"Weren't we all that way in high school?" Maxi asked.

"You can say that again," Claire sliced a small piece of cheesecake and bit in. It was the perfectly creamy blend of sweet raspberry and dark chocolate. Maybe she should consider hiring Maxi to supply some cheese-cakes for Sandcastles. *If* James would approve. "I think I have the marketing covered. I have a sign now out front and flyers on order."

"I heard about the sign," Jane said. She didn't quite meet Claire's gaze, her brow furrowing as she scooped out some of the dip with her cracker. It was loaded with pink chunks of succulent lobster. Urchin, still in Maxi's lap, lifted his head enough to eye the dip.

Claire smiled. "You did? That's great! It's already working."

The cracker hovered midway to Jane's mouth. Her eyes met Claire's. "Actually, I heard about it from the owner of Bradford Breads."

"Really? When did you talk to him?" Odd that Jane hadn't even mentioned knowing the guy. Well, there was probably nothing to it.

"Today. He came to Tides to see if we wanted to put in a standing order for fresh bread." Jane tucked her hair behind her ear and added, "He seems nice. He was very sweet to Mom."

Claire just bet he was. Probably trying to find out how easy it would be to take all of Claire's business through Jane somehow. But how would he even know they were friends? Claire thought about the man she'd seen going into Bradford Breads. "Was he tall? Fit? Graying around the temples?"

Jane brightened. "You've met already?"

"Not exactly. I saw him go into Bradford Breads earlier today, but he's not the owner. Probably a go-between or manager."

"No. The man I met is the owner. He said so. It's in his name too. Rob Bradford."

Could the man she had seen on the street be the owner of the rival bakery? No, the owner couldn't be that good-looking, or that down-to-earth, if his clothes and car had been any indication. Jane must have met someone else.

And sweet?

"Well, just because he was nice to Adelaide doesn't mean he's a good person. Who wouldn't be nice to an old lady?"

A shadow crossed in front of her friend's eyes. "You'd be surprised."

Uncomfortable, Claire shifted in her spot. She took a sip of wine. "Of course Bradford wants you to think he's nice. They always seem that way right before they put you out of business."

"He isn't going to put you out of business."

Claire snorted. Did Jane want to buy bread from the guy? She often got baked goods from Claire, and Claire knew that Jane was worried about Tides. Maybe she thought having fresh bread would help business. Claire didn't want to stand in the way of that.

"Do you think fresh bread would be good for the inn? You should try it." Claire tried not to sound stiff and frosty.

"I don't think I will just yet," Jane said immediately.

"But if it makes sense for the inn…"

"The inn has survived without fresh bread this long." Claire felt like Jane was passing on the proposition to be loyal to Claire because she saw Bradford Breads as a rival. The warmth of her friendship bloomed inside Claire's chest, at least until Jane added, "But you should give him a chance."

"Ummm, I don't think so."

Jane looked conflicted. "Honestly, he's not out to ruin your business."

"So he told you."

"I believe him." Jane rarely spoke with such conviction, even among friends. She was more apt to agree than butt heads. The mysterious Mr. Bradford must have made quite the impression. "He was actually worried when he saw the sign you were putting up outside."

Claire scoffed. "I bet he was! My sale is going to blow away his grand opening, and he knows it."

"You're selling different products. It's probably more reason for customers to visit you both. If you worked together to do more promotions like this, it could benefit you both. And he's willing to work together. You should at least talk to him and give him a chance."

Claire took a sip of wine and thought about it. Some of what Jane said made sense, but those old fears of failure crept up. What if Bradford Breads was just trying to get on her good side so he could figure out her vulnerabilities before he went in for the kill? Thoughts of Sandee just waiting for her to fail blurred her vision. Nope, she wasn't about to take a chance. Not right then, anyway.

She turned to Maxi. "What do you think, Maxi? I think Jane sees too much of the good in people sometimes."

Maxi had been in a world of her own, daydreaming about painting and sketching, so she was surprised when she heard her name. "Huh?"

"Earth to Maxi. Jane was suggesting that I team up with Bradford Breads. She thinks the owner is nice. I say he's up to something."

Maxi frowned at Jane. "How do you know the owner of Bradford Breads?"

"Have you not been listening at all? He came by the inn trying to set up an ongoing delivery for fresh bread."

"Oh, sorry. I guess I let my mind wander. That sounds like it could be advantageous to both of you."

Claire's tight-lipped smile indicated that she didn't agree, but Maxi knew that since both she and Jane were encouraging it, Claire would give it careful consideration.

"We'll see what happens after the grand opening and my cupcake sale." Claire forked up a piece of cheesecake and gestured toward Maxi with it. "This is excellent by the way."

"Thanks."

"So the advertising is underway, and we have a baking plan," Jane said. "Don't forget to get me some flyers."

Hailey looked over at the spreadsheet on Jane's

tablet. "If you fill out the spreadsheet and send it to me, I'll get the rest of the ingredients tomorrow morning, if you want me to, Claire."

Claire nodded.

Hailey stood. "Great. I'll see if Mrs. Pease can watch Jennifer for an extra hour each day. That way I can get a batch of cupcakes in before I leave work."

"Thanks. I'd appreciate that. As it is, I think I'll be living at Sandcastles. But at least no one else needs me at home." Claire narrowed her eyes at Urchin, who was still in Maxi's lap. "I'm not even sure Urchin will miss me."

"That has its advantages." Hailey bent to pick up her purse and the bag from Maxi. "No one to tell us what we can or can't do or disapprove of our plans."

"You can say that again. I remember Peter always had something negative to say about any of my dreams." Claire savored another bite of pie. "I wanted to open a bakery years ago, but he was against it. Good thing I got rid of him."

Hailey laughed. "Yeah, I got the same from Lance. The only time he relented was toward the end. Then he seemed to encourage anything I wanted. Of course, it turned out that was because he was cheating and wanted to distract me."

Claire laughed. "Same with Peter! Turns out he

was being nice and letting me do what I wanted to keep me busy so I wouldn't notice he'd taken up with Sandee."

Claire's words hit Maxi like a brick. *Keep me busy.* Wasn't that what James had said when he approved of her starting to draw again?

"Glad those days are past us." Hailey fist-bumped Claire. "Thanks for the gift, Maxi."

"Huh? Oh, you're welcome." Maxi's mind whirled as she watched Hailey leave. Surely, she was overreacting. The comment about keeping her busy was something anyone would say. But then she remembered how James had covered the phone. Who had he been talking to? She'd assumed he was in a break room or hallway at the convention, but maybe someone had been in his hotel room.

Maxi's thoughts were interrupted by a sputtering and coughing coming from the other side of the fence.

"What in the world?" Jane stood and peeked over. "Why is Hailey in a beat-up old Dodge? Thing looks like it's on its last leg. I thought she had a Toyota."

"She does." Claire had joined Jane at the fence, and Maxi dumped Urchin on the ground so she could look too.

The car was pulling away. Its rusted trunk looked ready to pop open. What was left of the paint was a faded gray. As they watched, a puff of smoke came out the back, and the car bucked.

"Is that thing safe?" Jane asked. "I hate to think of her driving Jennifer around in that."

"Me too. Maybe her car is in the shop," Maxi said.

"She goes to Frank's, and he has better loaners than that. I'll find out what the story is." Jane sat back down. Frank was her cousin and owned the best auto body shop in town.

"I hope she isn't having money troubles." Claire's expression showed genuine concern. "Maybe I should think about a raise, but Sandcastles needs a lot of repairs, and there's the competition across the street to be wary of."

Jane and Maxi exchanged a look. It was clear that Claire was still thinking of Bradford Breads as the competition, even though they'd both tried to dissuade her, but they both knew that pressing the matter would only make things worse.

Maxi held up her glass of wine. "All the more reason to make sure Sandcastles's cupcake sale is a rousing success."

CHAPTER THIRTEEN

*C*laire needed as many cupcakes as possible, so despite the fact that she had two helpers coming that evening, she started baking as soon as she could the day after their strategy meeting.

She began with the cupcakes she knew would sell the best, the flavors that flew off the shelves. Despite Sandee's disdain for them, chocolate and vanilla were crowd pleasers. Everyone loved them, and she consistently sold the most of them. She started with one batch of each. While they were baking in her industrial oven, she set a timer on her phone and went out front to help Hailey.

Mentally cataloguing all the things she had to do and in what order, Claire whisked away several errant dishes from customers who hadn't returned them to the front, wiping down the tables as she went. As she bent over one of the tables in front of the window, she smiled at Harry and Bert, sitting with their coffees in hand. They were drinking leisurely despite the clouds rolling in from the west.

"Good morning, gentlemen. Are you enjoying your coffees?"

"Always do," Bert said, tipping his up to take a sip from it.

"We can't wait for that cupcake sale," Harry added. "We saw the advertisement in the paper. Very classy."

"Thank you." She couldn't really take credit for that. Due to the last-minute rush for the ad, she hadn't been able to design anything and had left that to Mona. But Bert and Harry didn't need to know that.

"And the sign you have outside is quite something. I don't suppose you have samples of some of the flavors you'll be selling on Saturday?" Bert added.

Claire laughed. "Not today, I'm afraid. I've got plain old chocolate and vanilla in the oven right now. But if you come back tomorrow, I'll try to keep a small sample aside for two of my best customers."

The old men beamed. "We'll hold you to that," Harry said. Bert nodded in agreement.

As Claire straightened, her gaze was drawn to the stream of tourists walking past the banner that Stacy had made for the sale. She was pleased to see potential customers craning their necks to look. A few even stopped and headed inside despite the sign advertising a sale coming on Saturday. Claire's chest swelled at the sight of her bustling business. Getting Stacy to fast-track the sign had been the right decision.

The warm bubble in her chest burst as her gaze lifted from her cheery pink-and-yellow sign to the blatant red *Grand Opening* sign on the shop across the street. Claire chewed on the inside of her cheek and turned away. She had too much to do to start worrying about that.

As she headed into the kitchen area, balancing the dishes on her arms, Sally appeared from the hall that led to the bathrooms, where she had been fixing the leak. Claire slipped the dishes onto the counter next to the coffee and faced her.

"Finished?"

Sally nodded. "I think it should hold for a while."

Claire's shoulders relaxed with relief, but then she became wary of the smirk on Sally's face as the handy-woman's gaze travelled past her to the front of the store.

"Looks like you have company. I'm going to grab a coffee."

"Huh?" Claire turned as the bell above the door

chimed. Her gaze landed squarely on the man filling her doorway.

The guy from Bradford Breads. In *her* store. He paused in the threshold, letting the door fall back into its frame as he scanned the interior of the bakery. Was he examining her products? Trying to figure out how to best compete?

Wiping her hands on her apron, she left the safety of the kitchen area and headed out front. When he saw her, he smiled, the expression deepening the attractive crow's-feet at the corners of his sapphire eyes. She didn't return the smile.

Undaunted, he stepped forward to meet her halfway with a hand extended. "You must be the owner of Sandcastles."

Reluctantly, Claire slipped her hand into his. His palm was large and warm, with interesting callouses along the knuckles. She gave him a firm handshake, refusing to show even the slightest bit of weakness. Chin held high, she answered, "I am. Claire Turner."

"I'm Rob Bradford. I own the bakery across the street. Do you have a minute to talk?"

So, he *was* the owner. Claire hadn't wanted to believe Jane. She wanted the owner to be the soft, balding, work-avoiding guy that she envisioned getting out of his flashy red car with the blond trophy wife. This guy didn't look anything like that.

She took her phone out of her pocket, quickly checking the time left on the cupcakes she was baking. Seven minutes and counting. She stuffed the phone back into the pocket of her apron and looked Rob Bradford in the eyes, which—her brain happened to inform her, even though she really didn't want to know—were a pleasingly deep sapphire blue. "I only have seven minutes. Let's talk outside."

Something flashed across his face, indefinable and gone in an instant, but it left something niggling in the back of Claire's mind. The expression had reminded her of something, but she couldn't think of what.

The sky had darkened. Appropriate for their meeting, Claire thought as she led him to the farthest table she'd set out on the walkway and sat across from him. Her fingers itched for something to do. Rather than drum them on the table, she linked her hands together in front of her and resisted the urge to look at the timer on her phone.

He flashed her a charming smile that emphasized the cleft in his chin, and she got a funny feeling of déjà vu. "So, I suppose you've noticed that I'm opening soon."

Claire raised a brow. Did the guy think she was blind? "Of course. Is that why you came over?"

His smile faltered. Clearly he'd been expecting her to fall for his charms. The bakery owners that he'd surely put out of business in the other towns he'd infiltrated probably crumbled at those perfect teeth and the appealing crinkles around his eyes. He probably expected her to do the same and acquiesce to his plan for town dominance of baked goods.

Claire smiled inwardly knowing that her frosty response had thrown him off balance.

He cleared his throat. "I was thinking we should team up. If we combine our efforts, we could both benefit. Take the sale—there's no reason customers visiting the grand opening of my store won't want to step across the road and pick up a batch of cupcakes and vice versa. We can help one another."

Sure they could. Claire imagined how he would maneuver things in his favor. If they worked together, he would know more about her resources. He would be able to figure out ways to hurt her business. That wasn't going to happen, but she didn't want to let on that she was on to him—better to let him think she was naive and unaware of his plans.

With a tight smile, she told him, "I'll think about it. Right at the moment, though, I'm very busy."

He looked surprised at her bluntness. Frankly she couldn't blame him. She had come off a bit ruder than she'd intended. Oh well, better to let him know right off the bat that they were not going to be friends.

As she stood, he did too. He flashed her an uncertain smile. That time a dimple winked in and out of life in his left cheek, making him seem almost boyish. Something in his blue eyes, a twinkle, brought back memories.

It was *him*. Bobby from under the cedar tree. That one magical kiss of her youth that she'd never forgotten. He was standing right in front of her, thirty-five years later.

Memories of that night came rushing back to her, as if she were there again: the darkness sheltering their shyness and making them braver, her heart fluttering in her throat as she leaned into the kiss, the hope that she would see him again the next day, get to know him better, steal another kiss.

But then there was the bitter disappointment she'd felt at not finding him on the beach or in town the next day, the next night, all through the next week. She'd learned through a friend of a friend that he and his family had left Lobster Bay. Their vacation had ended. He hadn't said goodbye. He hadn't made contact with her again.

And even if their kiss had predated the days of
Facebook or cell phones and she'd been too swept up to
remember to give him her number, he could have found
her if he'd only put in a little effort. If anything, the
way he'd kissed her and left town without a second
thought only proved that he wasn't to be trusted.

She realized that she was standing in front of him,
gawking, not saying a word. He appeared to be too
absorbed in his own thoughts to call her on her peculiar
behavior. His forehead was wrinkled with concentration, that teasing look replaced with something else.
Something pensive.

He tucked his hands into his pockets, curling his
shoulders inward like he was a sheepish teenager.
"There's something familiar about you. Have we met
before?"

Panic surfaced. She couldn't let him know she
remembered. That might give him an advantage. And
maybe her pride was a bit wounded that he'd never
made an effort to contact her. She didn't want to give
him the satisfaction of knowing she remembered that
long-ago kiss.

She crossed her arms over her chest. "Have you
been to Lobster Bay before?"

"I have. It was a long time ago, when I was a

teenager. I vacationed here with my family. I think I met a girl named Claire."

"Really? Huh, I don't remember you, but there are a lot of girls named Claire. I'm sure it wasn't me."

He stared at her for a few more seconds then smiled again. "Sorry. You seemed familiar."

She cleared her throat and turned away. "If you'll excuse me, I have a business to run. I'll think about your offer to work together."

She managed to reach the door to her bakery without turning back to look at him, but as she opened it, the itch between her shoulder blades grew unbearable. She turned to pull the door shut behind her, taking the opportunity to look at him one more time. He stepped off the curb to cross the street, his strides long and confident. His polo shirt clung to his shoulders, framing the line of his body as he crossed smoothly toward his store on long legs.

One thing was for sure, he hadn't lost any of his good looks in the past thirty-five years. If anything, he'd filled out from the lanky teenager into a distinguished man who probably drew the eye of any woman with a pulse.

That included Sally, who lurked by the doorway, watching him leave, and made an appreciative sound under her breath. Claire sighed, then her brows snapped together.

What was burning?

Jerking the phone from her pocket, she checked her timer only to find that she had turned it on silent by accident. Her alarm had already gone off.

Oh no—my cupcakes!

❧

When Rob had left Lobster Bay on that last vacation thirty-five years ago, he'd been fresh with the memory of his first real kiss and eager to return and find that girl again. He'd kicked himself all the way home in the backseat of his parents' car for not asking for her phone number. But he'd been fifteen. He'd been nervous. He hadn't really known how to broach that subject or how his shy attempts at flirting had led to that one magical kiss.

Then his mom had gotten sick, and more important things had occupied his thoughts. But every once in a while, the memory would surface, and he would be looking into those gold-flecked hazel eyes again. The same eyes that Claire Turner had. He was positive Claire was the girl he had never forgotten, but apparently, she'd forgotten all about him.

She had changed. Her face and body had matured, but her eyes hadn't. And her auburn hair—he remembered that, too, though now it was shot through with silver—was the same rich color that shone like copper in the sunlight. How had he not recognized her from the second he saw her?

Now, more than ever, he wanted to work together with her. Meeting her again was a sign. He was doing the right thing moving to Lobster Bay, making his fresh start where he had some of his fondest memories.

And even though Claire didn't remember him, it might be like a second chance. The timing was right. He hadn't been able to even think about starting over with someone else after Caroline died, but now it was five years later. He was lonely. It was time. Claire didn't remember him, but that was okay. He wasn't fifteen anymore. He wasn't a nervous kid. He was a man who knew how to capture the attention of a woman.

If only she wasn't so intent on hating his guts.

CHAPTER FOURTEEN

*I*diot, *idiot, idiot.* As Claire tossed cupcake after cupcake into the trash, the refrain flashed across her mind. She shouldn't have even given Rob or Robbie or whatever his name was the time of day, let alone the more than ten minutes she'd allotted him. Where had the time gone? It seemed as though they'd been talking for only two or three minutes.

Two or three *tense* minutes.

Frustrated at finding every single one of the cupcakes she had in the oven charred, she upended the muffin tray and dumped them into the trash. Several bounced off the rim and scattered over the floor. As she bent to retrieve them, thunder rumbled in the distance. Her pipes creaked ominously in response, as if they were communicating with the building storm. Claire swore under her breath as she went on all fours to collect the chocolate cupcake that had rolled beneath the table she used for mixing and rolling. She fished it out and plopped it into the trash with the others.

She carried the muffin trays over to the sink to scrub away the charred remnants of cupcake batter. As the sink filled with hot, soapy water, her phone rang. Jane's name popped up as the phone continued to ring in her palm. Jane never called during business hours. She always texted.

A foreboding feeling pinched her gut as Claire answered the phone. "Jane?"

"Oh my God. Claire!" Jane's voice was thin and shrill. She sounded close to tears.

"I'm here. What's wrong?"

"Please tell me you've seen my mom."

"Addie? No. Why?" That feeling in Claire's gut pulled it into a tighter knot. "Did something happen?" In her heart, she already knew the answer.

"She's gone. I can't find her. Please, I need help."

"I'll be there in five minutes. Don't panic."

As Claire hung up the phone, she heard another peal of thunder. Without even bothering to take off her apron, Claire bolted for the front of the shop.

Hailey looked up at her, her forehead creased. "Claire? What is it?"

"I know you're about to leave, but I need you to stay on for a little while longer. There's been an emergency."

"An emergency?" The younger woman's eyes were round.

Claire swallowed and nodded, struggling to maintain her composure. Jane's panic had infected her. Addie would be fine. She had probably only wandered off to a spot where no one thought to look. But with the growing storm, that could be dangerous. If she'd wandered down to the beach... "Adelaide from Tides has wandered off. Jane is putting together a search group."

At least she assumed Jane was doing that. Jane couldn't search everywhere by herself. She'd called Claire, so she must have called Maxi too. Maxi had a head for organization. The first thing she would think of was organizing a search party. Even if that search party only consisted of Jane, Claire, Maxi, and Brenda. They would find Addie before anything bad happened. They had to.

"Go," Hailey said. "I'll call Mrs. Pease."

"If you can't stay, just close up shop. Business will be slow with a storm anyway."

Claire might lose a few sales, but this was much more important.

Despite the cold wind now whipping in from the ocean, Claire bolted for her Vespa.

Word must have spread fast, as a dozen people were already at Tides ready to help. Jane stood on the porch, one hand clutching the hood of her raincoat to her head, the other pointing in various directions as she organized the search. She vibrated with nerves, her eyes scanning the small group of people as they broke into pairs to search the grounds and beach. Claire parked her Vespa and joined Jane on the porch.

Fat raindrops had just started to fall. It was going to be an interesting ride back on the Vespa if the storm didn't blow through.

"What do you want me to do?"

Jane turned to her, despair clear on her face.

Claire enveloped her in a hug. "We'll find her. I promise. Where do you want me to look?"

Jane pushed herself taller, sniffling. "I don't know. Maxi took a group down to the neighbors on all sides to see if they've seen Mom. I want to go, too, but what if she comes back?"

Claire had never seen her friend look so lost, so helpless. She squeezed Jane's arm. "Staying here is a good decision. If she comes back, you can text us and let us know so we can too."

Jane swallowed hard. "With the storm, what if...?"

"We'll find her," Claire said with feeling.

"I've been sending people out in pairs, just in case something happens. You know how quickly thunderstorms can sweep up and how treacherous the beach can be, especially if there's lightning. I don't want anyone to go out alone. It's dangerous."

"Don't worry about me. I can go alone. In fact, I know where I want to look."

"Where is that?"

The male voice made the hairs on the back of Claire's neck stand on end. She hadn't realized that someone had come up behind them. She turned, back straight, to face Rob Bradford.

To her surprise, he looked as concerned as Jane was. Claire noticed the grateful look on her friend's face. Of course another hand in the search was welcome. She would have to set aside her feelings toward her competitor for Jane's sake. Finding Addie was the important thing.

Rob must have noticed the questioning look on Claire's face. "I heard about Adelaide in town. I want to help. I have experience with dementia."

He and Jane shared something unspoken, and she nodded.

When Jane turned to her, Claire was proud of the confidence she projected, even if the truth was far from it.

"You'll go with Claire, then. Claire, you don't mind?"

"It's fine," she said without looking at the man standing next to her. She pushed her hair out of her eyes. "Let's go. We're wasting time standing here." She turned, taking off down the beach without waiting for him.

Rob fell into step beside her without question. "Where to?"

"Addie used to take Claire and me to the beach all the time as children. There's a spot just north of here, a pool in low tide where we would find small fish, hermit crabs, seashells, that sort of thing. It's cut off from the ocean itself by this rocky shore, so we weren't in danger of getting swept out to sea. We'd go every week, sometimes more often."

As Claire spoke, she was already leading him away from the white Victorian house and down the narrow path to the beach below. She hadn't visited that pool since she was a teenager, preferring to walk on the beach or along the Marginal Way. The spot was close enough to Tides for the community to consider it Adelaide's property and tucked in between dunes and rocky outcrops, which discouraged tourists.

Thunder rumbled overhead, and the ocean spat fingers of spray at them. It slickened the rocks over which she led Rob, who neither complained nor hovered at her elbow like an overprotective mother duck. At the bottom of the path, they came to a crude footbridge of flat wooden boards. The bridge crossed over the dunes to the alcove where the pool lay.

Rain pummeled them, soaking Claire's hair and sending bedraggled strands in front of her eyes. At least she'd thought to put on her raincoat. Despite the pounding in her heart, she moved more slowly, testing each foot in front of the other. Between the sheets of rain, she squinted, hoping to see a familiar figure.

What if Adelaide wasn't there? What if no one found her in time and she was washed out to sea?

Lightning split the sky, sharpening the dim scenery. Not far, on a flat rock overlooking the pool, a shadow moved.

"Addie!"

Claire bolted for the pool, waving her hands for balance as she navigated the slippery rock-lined path that had changed in subtle ways since she was a girl. The entire time, she never looked away from that shape.

It resolved into Adelaide sitting on the rock with her shoulders hunched and her knees to her chest like a little girl. She'd lost one of her shoes. The other one hung impotently from her toe. When she saw Claire, she reared back, startled.

Claire stopped. Rain drizzled down the back of her neck into her shirt. The chill made her shiver. "Addie, it's me, Claire. Jane is looking for you. It's time to come home."

Addie looked at Claire as if she didn't know her. What was she supposed to do? She didn't want to scare Addie, but the tide was coming in fast, and the rain would only make the path more treacherous.

Rob knelt at Addie's feet, putting his head at the same level as hers. "What did you do to your foot?" His voice was soft, warm, patient despite the rain pelting down on him.

"I stepped on a rock and lost my shoe. Does it look bad?" Addie's voice was small.

"Let me see." Slowly, he stretched out his arm, watching the old woman for cues that she might bolt. When he touched her naked foot, she jerked it back but otherwise showed no signs of fear.

Only then did Claire notice the gash in the bottom of Addie's foot. How much worse could it have been if they hadn't found her?

"Nothing a Band-Aid won't fix," Rob pronounced.

Claire was fairly certain he was lying. The cut looked deep enough to need stitches.

"But we need to get you home first. If you can't walk, will you let me carry you?"

Adelaide looked at him through lowered lashes, shy. "I'm sure I'm too heavy for you."

He laughed. "A little bird like you?"

Addie glanced up at him from under her lashes. Despite the cut, it didn't seem to be hurting her too much. Claire couldn't decide if that was a good thing or a bad thing. Her heart was in her throat, and she was afraid to speak, afraid to confuse the old woman further.

She certainly couldn't carry her, but Rob could. And he was so good with her, so kind and patient. Jane hadn't been lying about that. This sort of thing, it wasn't the kind of thing someone could fake.

"I suppose if you *want* to carry me…"

"I can think of no greater honor," Rob teased. He stood, scooping Adelaide into his arms as he did. She let out a squeak and wrapped her bony arms around his neck.

He turned to Claire. His thoroughly soaked shirt stuck to his body. Raindrops snaked down his face, but even the dark afternoon from the cloudy overhead sky couldn't snuff out the brilliance of his eyes. He was calm, in control. "Are you okay making your way back to the inn on your own? I think it's better if I run."

"Of course," Claire said, stepping back without thinking. She met his gaze for a moment more before he took off. Adelaide whooped, the sound almost swallowed by a fresh peal of thunder. Dimly, Claire heard her shout something about jealousy and someone named Sadie Thompson.

They were gone before Claire started to move. She couldn't run as fast, but with the rain splattering her at every turn, she moved as quickly as she dared. She kept her eyes peeled for Addie's other shoe but didn't find it. She cradled the first between her hands and followed in Rob's wake, wondering if she might have misjudged him after all.

And what had he meant when he'd said he had "experience" with dementia?

CHAPTER FIFTEEN

R ain pelted the sides of the bed-and-breakfast. Outside, flashes of lightning reflected off the wavy glass of the old windows. Thus far, the power had held, but in a house as old as Tides, Claire wasn't holding her breath.

Everyone who had participated in the search had been contacted and accounted for. Some had gone, but a small crowd remained, clustering in the gathering room at the back of the inn, the only room big enough to accommodate that many people. Brenda had put together a platter of grapes, cheese, and crackers. It sat next to a pot of coffee on the table facing the wide windows looking out to the ocean.

Everyone's attention was on Addie. She sat in an oversized armchair, a heavy navy striped blanket tucked around her. She looked very small, like a child being tended to by her mother, as Jane knelt at her feet to examine the cut. The first aid kit was laid out next to her, bandages and gauze scattered haphazardly and spilling over the white plastic sides.

Kneeling next to Addie, with a towel hanging around his neck, Rob held her hand and spoke to her, keeping her calm as Jane tended to her foot. His messy wet hair made him look as if he'd just stepped from the shower. Now why in the world was she having thoughts like that?

As if he could feel her gaze, Rob looked up and smiled at her. Claire smiled back before she could catch herself. Rob was very attentive to Addie and had seemed concerned about the woman, but Claire warned herself not to be fooled. It was hard to fit this facet of him against that of the ruthless bakery owner she'd built up in her head, but people often acted nice when they had ulterior motives.

Not wanting to stare at him, Claire moved to the window, popped a grape in her mouth and poured a cup of coffee. The rain was starting to let up, thankfully. Claire didn't relish the idea of taking the Vespa back to Sandcastles. She could ask someone for a ride, but then she would have to walk back down and get it later.

She was on her third grape when a dry towel was

thrust into her arms. "Here," Rob said unceremoniously. "You look like you could use this."

"Thank you." She put the coffee down, wrapped the towel around her shoulders, and started drying her hair with the end.

Rob tucked his hands into his pockets, reminding her again of that fifteen-year-old boy she'd kissed decades ago. "I'm glad you made it back safely."

"I know the beach pretty well, so it wasn't that hard." Had she sounded bitchy? She didn't mean to, but she also didn't want to encourage a friendship with the guy.

"Of course." Rob glanced around. Jane had finished bandaging Addie and was packing up the first aid kit. "I'd better see if Jane wants my help moving Adelaide to another room."

Claire was staring after him as a familiar feminine voice asked, "Who's the cutie?"

She jumped.

Next to her, Maxi laughed. She hadn't even noticed her come up. "I knew I caught you staring."

"I was not staring. I was watching Jane with her mom."

"Sure you were." Maxi started toweling off her hair. "So who is he?"

"You don't know? It's the Bradford Breads guy."

Maxi's left brow hiked. "Ohhh, well at least he has appropriately nice buns."

"Maxi!" Claire exclaimed, but it emerged half as a choked laugh, no doubt her friend's intention.

"So you two aren't enemies anymore?" Maxi asked.

"I wouldn't say that. We had to pair up to find Addie at Jane's request. He's still under suspicion as far as I'm concerned."

Maxi's lips pressed together. "Really? He seems so nice to Addie, and didn't I hear that he found her and ran back through the storm carrying her? That's kind of a nice thing to do, especially as a newcomer."

"Maybe he has an ulterior motive." Claire's voice was missing some of the conviction she'd felt earlier.

"What would that possibly be? To befriend Jane so he can ruin your bakery?" Maxi curled her towel around her shoulders and poured a cup of coffee. "Don't you think you're reaching a bit?"

Claire chewed her bottom lip and studied her friend. Why did no one see things the way she saw them? There was only kindness and concern in Maxi's eyes. She wasn't being mean or malicious, but it wasn't *her* bakery that was in jeopardy. "I don't think I'm reaching. I tell you the guy is acting nice but there's something odd about it. Why does he dote on Addie so much? That doesn't seem normal to me."

Maxi shrugged. "Well, he has a soft spot for people with memory issues because of his wife."

"Wife?" Claire hadn't even thought about him having a wife, but of course he probably did. She hadn't seen any wife hanging around the store across the street. Where was she, and what did that have to do with Addie? "That makes it even stranger. Where is his wife?"

Maxi looked at her funny. "She died. I heard him mention it earlier. Didn't realize he was the bread guy. You didn't hear him talking about that to Jane when he brought Addie in?"

Claire shook her head. It must have been when she was still making her way back from where they'd found Addie.

"Oh, well apparently his wife had early-onset Alzheimer's." Maxi's face turned sad. "He took care of her while she was sick."

Something inside Claire softened. She glanced back at Rob, who had moved Addie to the couch and was still doting on her.

Loudly, Addie's voice cut through the murmur of people. "Stop fussing around me. I'm fine."

"Take it easy, Mom. You can't walk on that foot for a while."

"Stop coddling me. All of you go on now. I have an

inn to run! I can't sit around all day."

If nothing else, she sounded back in her usual spir-its. After the scare they'd had, it was a relief.

Claire sipped the last of her coffee. The rain had stopped. She'd better say goodbye to her friends and head back to the bakery. She had a cupcake sale to prepare for.

❀

By the time Maxi checked her phone, she found not one but three text messages from James.

The first had come not long after she had sent her initial text about Addie going missing. Jane's family was a pillar of the community, and she thought he would want to know that she was missing and that Jane was organizing half the town to look for her. The second text must have come in while Maxi was out knocking on neighbors' doors in search of Addie. And when she hadn't answered that…

Maxi, please text me back to let me know you are okay.

He cared. Maxi had started to wonder about that. Especially after what Claire and Hailey had said about their exes. Clearly she had too much time on her hands now, and it was making her overthink things. She leaned against the wall and tapped out a response immediately.

I'm fine. A bit wet. Claire found Addie and we're all inside now, warming up.

When she hit send, she tucked the phone against her and smiled, releasing a long breath and all of the tension that had gripped her those past few hours since she'd gotten Jane's call.

Most people had left, including Claire, who had toweled off the seat of her Vespa, shrugged on her raincoat, and zoomed off. Addie was sitting contentedly on the couch, talking to Rob Bradford. As she watched, Addie let out a carefree laugh in response to something Rob had said.

Maxi had been surprised to discover the good-looking stranger was the man Claire had built up to be some sort of dough-rolling villain. Claire hadn't mention that he was cute or that he had a kind way about him.

With a sigh, Maxi shook her head. How long was Claire going to hold onto this nonexistent animosity? To the outside eye, it was obvious that Rob held no ill will toward Claire. In fact, from the way he looked at her, he might even be smitten.

They would make a good couple. Both passionate about baking, they had a common interest. Claire had gotten a bit flustered when she'd tried to dismiss Rob's attractiveness. Maxi knew her friend too well. Claire *did* think Rob Bradford was cute. She was simply too scared, and too busy protecting her territory, to acknowledge that he might be worth pursuing.

Neither Claire nor Jane had dated in years, although Jane's reason was different. She'd been widowed quite suddenly. Maxi repressed a shudder, thinking how horrible it would be if she lost James. Maxi wanted her friends to be happy, but that didn't necessarily mean they needed a man in their lives.

But if Claire decided not to date again, it shouldn't be because of the hateful way her ex-husband had treated her. Maxi was certain she saw a spark between Claire and Rob.

Was there something she could do to help them over that initial hump? Probably not. Claire was as stubborn as a lobster sometimes. But even if nothing came of it, Maxi wished she could figure out a way to show Claire that Rob wasn't her enemy. In fact, he seemed like an all-around nice guy, and those types of people were hard to find.

The phone chimed again in her hand, and Maxi glanced down at the screen. She smiled at the words greeting her. Warmth spread through her, chasing out the lingering cold of the storm.

I'm glad you're safe. I love you.

She tapped out the reply on reflex. *I love you too.*

❀

Jane was putting up a brave front, but Rob knew from personal experience how upsetting it was to have a loved one wander off.

"Honestly, I don't think I can thank you enough for what you've done."

"It wasn't me. I carried your mother here, but the person who found her is Claire."

"It took both of you. And thanks for being so nice to her. I appreciate you distracting her while I bandaged the cut. She might have been hard to handle otherwise." Jane hugged herself and glanced at Addie, now seated calmly on the couch.

"Is the bandage enough? I could help you take her to the emergency clinic," Rob offered. The gash in Addie's foot hadn't looked half as bad once it was cleaned out, but it was best to be on the safe side.

"Norma Barnes looked at it. She's a nurse. She said it didn't need stitches, so I think we'll be okay." Jane hugged herself tighter and shivered. "I'm sorry I'm such a wreck about this."

Rob clasped her shoulder. "This was a big deal.

Taking care of someone is a lot of pressure. It's okay to be a wreck sometimes."

When Jane looked at him, her eyes shone with unshed tears. "This isn't the first time we've lost track of her. She gets so confused and I—I thought I had all my bases covered, that she was safe."

"This isn't your fault."

Jane looked away. "I guess I wasn't paying close enough attention to her."

Softly, he confessed, "I know how you feel. Believe me, I don't envy your position or the decisions you'll have to make, but you're strong enough to handle this. Today was a bad day. There are still good days."

Rob sympathized with her, and he was surprised he wasn't spiraling into all the complicated feelings about Caroline's illness. Maybe time really was starting to heal those wounds. It helped that Addie was older. Rob could separate her failing mind from that of his late wife, who had had her entire life ahead of her. Caroline had been his best friend, and he'd lost that long before he'd lost the empty shell her body had become. He managed on his own, but he missed having that connection with someone.

His thoughts turned to Claire and how determined she'd been to find Addie. He knew she still didn't trust him, but she'd set that aside because she wanted to help

Jane. Claire was a good friend. If nothing more, he could use good friends like that. But how to win her over?

"Do you think there are still good days? Because sometimes, I'm not so sure." Jane's question tugged him out of his thoughts.

"Of course there are."

Jane sighed. "Sometimes, I really don't know what to do. When she's having a good day, she's almost like her old self. A little forgetful maybe but not scaring me like this."

"I know," Rob said softly. He infused those two words with all the sympathy he could muster. He understood all too well how she felt in her position.

Quietly, she confessed, "She's afraid I'm going to put her in a home. She's mentioned it before and broken down because of it. I don't know what to do." Her eyes bleak, she raised them to meet Rob's. "What did you do for your wife?"

Rob hesitated. He rarely talked about the details of his wife's illness if he could help it. Jane had asked him earlier how he knew so much about dementia, and he'd simply told her he'd gone through the whole thing with his wife. But he knew the exact turmoil Jane was experiencing, and he wanted to help her.

At his hesitation, Jane apologized. "I don't mean to

pry. It's just so hard to know what's the right thing to do, but I don't want to dredge up unhappy memories for you. You've gone through more than you should have had to."

Normally, Rob grimaced at that answer. Pity was one thing he didn't need or want. But a shadow in her eyes made him wonder if she was echoing a sentiment she'd been trying to teach herself.

"I have," he answered. His gaze drifted, this time to Adelaide. "But so have you. I didn't put my wife in an assisted living facility."

Jane nodded briskly. "So, I'm doing the right thing in keeping her here."

"Not necessarily."

Was it a trick of the light, or did something like hope flit through her expression that time? She was tired. She wanted some relief. He knew exactly how that felt.

He told her, "I *should* have put Caroline in an assisted living or memory care facility. She asked for it, but I—I was selfish. I wanted to hold onto her for as long as possible." His left thumb travelled to meet his ring finger, where he no longer had his wedding ring. Sometimes, it surprised him to find it in the box in his nightstand instead of on his finger. Most days, he'd stopped thinking about it at all. "I was in a different position than you. I can work from home and only need to connect with my store managers in person once a week at most. And I had the money to hire a nurse to come in twice a day to care for her and sit with her while I did office work from home. I wasn't trying to run an inn. My managers are self-sufficient."

Jane hugged herself again, but she seemed to consider his words at the very least.

He added, "Ultimately, I kept her at home until the end. But I did extensive research into memory care facilities nearby. I'm happy to help you if you need it. I've been exactly in your shoes, and I don't think it's necessarily a bad thing to put your mother somewhere safe where she'll be lovingly cared for all the time."

Jane let out a gusty sigh, blowing the strands of hair falling into her face. "Maybe. I know she doesn't want it, but maybe it would be better to put her in a place where she'd have proper care. It… she scared me today. And I can't run the inn and be with her twenty-four hours a day."

"It looks like she scared a lot of people." He gave Jane's arm one last squeeze. "Let me sort out where I put all those pamphlets and emails, and I'll bring the information later this week."

Her smile only halfway reached her eyes, but the weight of the afternoon seemed to have lifted. "Thank you. I really don't know what I would have done without you today."

"Me and Claire," he reminded her. "We'd make a better team than she thinks."

Jane rolled her eyes. "So it seems, but it's going to take a bit of work to convince Claire of that."

CHAPTER SIXTEEN

The next morning, Claire was buzzing around the bakery, trying to get ahead of the regular chores so she could get in some extra cupcake baking. After the search for Addie, she'd returned to Sandcastles and, with the help of Sarah and Aston, had baked well into the night. Now she was standing in front of the fridge, taking an inventory of the cupcakes and trying to block out all distractions as she counted.

"I think it would do you some good."

Sally's voice buzzed distantly behind Claire. She shut the fridge door and wiped her tired eyes. The handywoman stood, leaning against the counter, chewing on a corn muffin slathered in butter, and dripping crumbs onto the top of her overalls.

"What are you talking about?"

The old woman swallowed then gestured through the air between them with half of the muffin left. "You and Bradford. It would do you good to work together, like he wants."

"Who told you he wanted that?"

"He did."

"He did? When did you talk to him?" Sally knew Rob Bradford? That was news to Claire. And why was he telling everyone that he wanted to work with her? It was odd that he was being so obvious and insistent about it. Clearly he was up to something.

"He's hiring local folks to fix some odds and ends in the store before the grand opening, so naturally he called me."

Claire glanced toward the front of the store, over the heads of the seated customers, and out the window to Bradford Breads. So, he'd hired her handywoman, eh? Probably thought he could get insider information. "What did you tell him about Sandcastles?"

Sally's face scrunched. "Tell him? What are you talking about? I fixed some trim that had come loose on the doorframe over there."

"Did he ask you questions about Sandcastles?"

"Yeah, he asked if I thought you'd be willing to work with him. Didn't I just say that?"

Claire sighed. "I mean specifics. Like maybe what our busiest day is or what pastry we sell the most of."

Sally took her time chewing the bite of muffin. "Nope. Why would he want to know any of that?"

Good question. What would he gain from getting insider information on Sandcastles? Claire wasn't sure. But then again, she wasn't exactly up on the various goals and objectives of corporate espionage. Rob Bradford probably was, though. People didn't get bakery chains by being naive about business.

Sally was still looking at her like she wanted an answer, but Claire was saved from having to answer by the pipes in the bathroom, which decided to let out a series of disturbing gurgles.

"Are you sure the patch on the pipes will hold? I've been hearing some gurgling." As if to punctuate that sentence, someone flushed the toilet in the café washroom, and the gurgling noises intensified. Fearfully, Claire stared at the wall, picturing a geyser erupting at any minute. She really hoped that didn't happen. She only had one public washroom, and if something in there broke, she would have to close the shop per town regulations. And if she had to close the shop, she wouldn't be able to make the cupcakes.

Sally popped the last of her muffin into her mouth and chewed. She shrugged and swallowed. "I don't know. You heard what Ralph said about the pipes, but gurgling doesn't have much to do with leaking. The patch should hold. Whether or not you'll have another leak…" Sally shrugged to indicate she couldn't make a prediction on that.

Right, well at least Sally wasn't expounding on how she should team up with Rob Bradford anymore. To distract herself, Claire set back to work. Even though it was early in the day, she wanted to get setup for the evening's baking. That way they could get started as soon as possible. She had time to make up for after yesterday.

"Flour, sugar, eggs, cocoa…" she muttered under her breath, listing the things she needed to bake the cupcakes.

She puttered toward the cupboards that housed her ingredients in pursuit of the first one. She pulled out the flour canister. It was empty. There were no helpfully stacked bags waiting next to it. She and her helpers had used all her flour last night.

Fortunately, she had thought ahead and sent in an order to her supplier for yesterday's delivery. She'd found it on the back doorstep when she had returned from Tides and tugged it into the shop before drying herself off and preparing for her helpers to come for the night's baking. They'd used up most of the flour she'd already had on hand and would need the new batch for tonight. Where had she put it?

She scanned the kitchen until she spotted the cardboard box with its distinctive logo on the side. Sunshine Flour was a US-based company that had the best flour she'd ever used. She lifted the box on the counter and took out a kitchen knife to break the seal of the delivery sticker on top.

The ink on the sticker was smudged. Claire had a sick feeling but ignored it as she cut into the sticker, which was dry, and the tape beneath. The box had been delivered yesterday while she was searching for Addie during the storm. Hailey, who hadn't been able to stay after all, due to a conflict in her babysitter's schedule, had manned the front only until the last customer had run to their car to drive home before the storm got worse. With the rain pouring down in sheets, Hailey had texted that she doubted Claire would be losing customers and she had to rush home to be with Jennifer before her babysitter left. She hadn't checked the back door before closing, and Claire had been too frazzled to remind her.

The cardboard beneath the tape wasn't moist exactly, but it didn't feel as sturdy as it should have. Claire reached inside the box to lift the first of the bags of flour stacked neatly on their sides to fit as many as possible into the box. The paper bag was still damp.

"Oh no."

She hefted the heavy bag and tore open the contents. It was wet and clumpy. Ruined. This wasn't good. She might not have enough flour to bake the cupcakes tonight.

"What's the matter?" Sally asked.

"The flour got wet."

It was one bag. Maybe the others...

She opened another bag. Ruined. A third. Ruined. That left only two. Even if they were both fine, she had to bake at least ten dozen cupcakes tonight, or she would fall too far behind to be ready for the sale.

"Why don't I run down to the grocery store and fetch you a few more bags?"

The offer was sweet, but Claire shook her head. "I don't buy my flour from the grocery store. I buy it from a specialty supplier. They have a pastry blend that is extremely soft and fine. I can't use grocery store flour, or the cupcakes won't have the same quality my customers are used to. I'll order more, but it will take at least a day to get here, and I have part-time help coming tonight to bake, and—"

Sally patted her arm. She had a kind face. Somehow, the crumb clinging to the corner of her mouth made her all the more sympathetic. "Is that the brand?" She tapped the side of the box.

Claire nodded. "Sunshine Flour."

A gleam entered Sally's eyes, and she stepped back with a sly smile. "Then I know exactly where to get you some. That Rob Bradford had a stack of these same flour bags in his shop. I'm sure he'd agree to let you borrow some if I asked."

"No, don't—"

Claire was too late. Sally had already turned and rushed out the door, leaving Claire with the unmistakable feeling that the day was about to turn into even more of a headache.

❧

Rob frowned at the trim old handywoman who stared up at him expectantly. "You want to borrow a cup of flour?" Granted, it was the neighborly thing to do, but as a bakery, he'd never precisely been asked. It looked like Lobster Bay was going to keep him on his toes.

Sally hooked her thumbs in the straps of her overalls. "Ayuh, well, I was thinking more like several bags. It's for Claire, across the road."

"Really?" Rob's gaze skipped to Sandcastles. Claire

had sent Sally over to borrow flour? What an interesting turn of events.

"Claire's shipment of flour got wet because, with all the hoopla going on up at Tides, the delivery was left outside in the rain. She's fresh out of flour, and they don't make emergency deliveries, so she'd have to wait until tomorrow." Sally leaned closer. "She's got all those cupcakes to make for the bake sale, and she needs that flour tonight."

Rob's smile widened. She needed the flour for the sale? This could be exactly the thing that would win Claire over.

"I'd be happy to bring over some flour for Claire. She needs one bag?"

"I'd say closer to three. She lost at least three in her shipment, and she has part-time help coming over this evening to bake."

Perfect. Lending her flour for that would surely show her that he had no ill will toward her bakery. "Why don't I lend her four bags just to be sure she has enough? They're heavy. I'll carry them across the street for you."

Sally was robust. As a handywoman, she kept in pretty good shape despite her age. Rob had seen her carry some pretty heavy boards around. Nevertheless, a sneaky smile spread across her face. "What a great idea. I'm sure I couldn't carry all four."

In the end, Sally lugged one bag while he carried the other three. She led him around the building to the door on the side of Sandcastles, which opened directly into the kitchen.

As he stepped inside, he noticed the kitchen was old but had a rustic charm. The sweet smell of cookies hit his nose, and his stomach grumbled.

The color was high in Claire's cheeks as she turned from where she'd been pulling the cookies out of the oven. She had an apron tied around her waist, and he noticed that it accentuated her curves. He forced himself to look her in the eye as he gallantly offered her the bags of flour.

"I hope four is enough for your purposes."

"I don't want to put you out. I wasn't going to ask to borrow any, but *someone*"—she glanced at Sally over Rob's shoulder—"ran off before I could stop her. I mean, it's not like I'm so unprepared that I need to borrow flour."

So Claire hadn't sent Sally over on purpose? Darn, for a minute there he'd thought he'd made some progress with the feisty baker.

Rob set the bags of flour down on the counter. "It's no trouble. I had extra. Sally told me yours got wet."

Claire nodded. "In the storm yesterday."

"Right."

Tension hummed in the air between them, and Rob was uncertain what to say. Here was a great opportunity to broach the subject of the sale and the possibility of working together, but the frown on Claire's face stopped him.

Sally was watching them like a hawk watching a wounded baby rabbit. "Claire has that big cupcake sale on Saturday. You have your big opening then, don't you, Rob?"

"I do." What was Sally up to? Rob supposed he didn't mind. He could use the help since he wasn't doing a good job himself.

"Well, since you're both trying to get customers down here and you're set up across the street from each other…"

"I hardly think people will want to shop in both stores, if that's what you're getting at." Claire peeled the oversized cookies off the tray with a rubber spatula and set them carefully on a cooling rack. They were golden brown with sugar crystals on top. Rob's mouth watered.

"I disagree." Sally reached for a cookie, touching it tentatively to see if it was too hot. "I think after choosing the bread they're going to have at supper or keep in the kitchen for sandwiches, people are going to want to relax with a coffee and pastry. You guys could cross-promote. Would be better for both of you."

Claire hesitated, and for a moment, Rob thought she might be considering it. "That might have been a good idea a few weeks ago, but now there are only two days, and it's just not enough time to set anything up. Besides, all my time is taken between now and then. I don't have time to plan anything. Unlike some people, I can't just leave my shop willy-nilly." Claire shot Rob a pointed look.

Ouch! The only reason he could leave was because the shop wasn't open yet. Once it was, he would be tied to it as much as Claire was tied here. Even though he owned a chain of stores, he worked just as hard as anyone, especially in this particular store since he would be the manager. But he could tell that Claire had made up her mind. There would be no point in pushing because that would only make her dig her heels in more.

He raised his hands in surrender. "You might be right. There isn't a lot of time to make a plan. I hope the flour helps."

Claire's demeanor softened. Almost reluctantly, as if the words were dragged from her, she murmured,

"Thank you for the flour, and that was a nice thing you did for Addie yesterday."

Rob shoved his hands in his pockets, suddenly self-conscious. "It was nothing really. I mean, I know how heart-wrenching it is when a loved one wanders off, so when I heard she'd gone missing, I had to volunteer to help. Plus, I'd met Addie the day before, and she's a real firecracker. I would hate to think of her coming to any harm."

Claire nodded. They were silent as her gaze held his for just a fraction of a second. In that fraction, Rob felt like he'd made some progress.

Sally broke the silence, her voice pointed. "Rob is widowed."

Despite his resolve to keep his past to himself, he'd found himself opening up to the town handywoman enough to tell her that much. But why was she blurting that out now?

Claire shot Sally a look then muttered. "I'm sorry about that."

"Claire is divorced."

Color washed into Claire's cheeks. "Sally!"

The old woman grinned, seemingly pleased with herself. "I thought you ought to know. To make it easier to work together. No jealous wives or husbands around to grumble if you two need to work late."

Surprisingly bashful, Claire turned away. She didn't look at Rob.

Rob glanced at Sally. Sally winked and reached for another cookie.

"I should get back to my shop. I have a lot of prep to do before Saturday." Rob turned to leave through the back door.

"Thanks again for the flour," Claire said.

He turned to catch her eye one last time, but she was already pulling bowls out of a cupboard, her back to him. "It's my pleasure," Rob said. "If you ever need anything, I'm right across the street."

As Rob walked back over to his shop, he couldn't keep from smiling. Even though Claire still didn't want to work with him, he could tell he'd made some progress. It was going to be a challenge to break through Claire Turner's tough shell, but he had a feeling it would be worth it.

CHAPTER SEVENTEEN

*D*espite the late-summer sunset, darkness had fallen by the time Claire squeezed the last of the cupcakes into her fridge and shut the door. She waved wearily to Sarah, tugging the side door shut behind her so it would latch. Ashton would be leaving, too, after he cleaned up in the bathroom, but it was a habit to keep that door closed. She really should have Sally fix it soon.

Her feet aching, she lowered herself onto a stool and leaned her elbows onto the table. Sarah had wiped it down before leaving, and all three of them had done the dishes while the last batch of cupcakes was in the oven. Claire was eager to get home. Poor Urchin would be frantic for his dinner.

The toilet flushed, and water gurgled through the

pipes. Claire made a face. The pipes had been groaning all night, as if they were haunted. She didn't need that nightmare—or the reminder of replacing them. She'd contacted the bank about a small loan, but there was so much paperwork. She had no time to look at it.

The pipes hissed alarmingly, followed by a thunk and a muffled curse. A second later, Ashton stepped into the kitchen. His shoes squeaked on the floor, leaving a wet trail. He looked apologetic, wringing his hands. "I swear I didn't do anything, Ms. Turner. It just started leaking on its own."

"A leak?" *Crap!*

"It's coming from under the sink in the bathroom. I don't know how to fix it."

"It's fine," she assured him. She must have a good poker face because he relaxed. If only she really did feel it was fine. "I'll give Sally a call. She can fix it." Or so Claire hoped. Was it the same place she'd already fixed, and if so, could someone even fix something like that twice?

Claire took a deep breath. It was still two days until the sale. Hopefully that was enough time to fix it, even if it needed something more than a patch. But still, she couldn't have the bathroom out of commission at all because then the store would be shut down, and who would want to come to a cupcake sale at a place that had been shut down for two days?

Ashton was staring at her. "So I can go home?"

"Yes. Go home. I'll see you tomorrow."

He didn't wait to hear her say it again. He was out the door before she pulled her phone out of her apron pocket.

She dialed Sally, holding her breath as she approached the bathroom. Hopefully, she could convince Sally to work on it tonight. Timidly, Claire pushed open the door. The hiss was louder in there, the water pooling out from beneath the sink at an alarming rate. *Oh no!*

She bent down to look underneath. How in the world did one make this thing stop running?

Come on, Sally. Pick up!

"Hello?"

Claire blew out a breath of relief upon hearing Sally's voice. "Sally, I have a problem at the shop." Her voice was high and shakier than she'd hoped. She swallowed hard.

"A problem?" A garble in the background pulled Sally's attention from the phone. "Hush, honey. I'll be done in a minute." Then closer again. "What's the problem?"

"A leak. In the bathroom."

"Where is it coming from?"

"Under the sink."

"Same spot as before?"

"I think so."

"You *think*?"

Claire crouched down to take another look. "It's kind of hard to tell with water spraying everywhere." Just then, even more water gushed out. She pulled away, leaving the door wide open. The water spewed from the cabinet to the growing puddle on the floor.

Claire ran to the kitchen and grabbed some towels. "Definitely the same place. How do I turn this thing off?"

"Turn the valve."

Claire dropped the towels on the floor. They became soaked immediately. "Valve?"

"It's easy. Look under the sink. There's a knob on the side of the pipe that leads from the sink to the floor. Find it and turn it."

Afraid of her phone getting wet, Claire thumbed the button to turn the call onto speaker and put it on the vanity counter. Taking a deep breath, she stuck her head inside the cabinet. Cold water splashed over her arm and down her front as she groped for the knob.

She found it. Turned. The knob stopped with a creak. "It's not working. I think it's getting worse!"

"It can't get worse. The water is either on or it's off. Turn it the other way."

Claire did so, her hand slipping over the cold metal before she got a firm grip. As she turned it as far as possible in the other direction, the fountain of water slowed and then stopped. Claire sat back on her heels. She was soaked, but she'd stopped the water.

Except now there was no water to the sink. And no water meant no bathroom for the customers. She needed Sally to get there to fix it.

"I did it. The water stopped. How soon can you get here to fix the leak?"

The pause on the other end of the line made Claire's stomach roil. She took the call off speaker, held the phone to her ear, and swished the towel around with her foot to sop up some of the water.

"Sally?"

"Well, I can't make it there tonight."

"What?"

"I'm in Portland babysitting my grandson. I won't return to Lobster Bay until tomorrow afternoon."

"*Afternoon?*" Claire had held out a faint hope of Sally sneaking in early in the morning to fix the problem before the shop opened. But without the bathroom fixed, Claire might not be able to open her shop tomorrow at all.

"You could call Ralph."

Claire pushed out a breath. Ralph's hourly rate spiked to unaffordable after five p.m., but what choice did she have? "I will. Thanks."

Claire hung up and glared at the faulty pipes. "Why couldn't you have stayed fixed for just a few more days?"

"Who are you talking to?"

The voice made her jump. Heart pounding, she turned to see Rob Bradford standing in the doorway. She bristled. "You almost gave me a heart attack! What are you doing here?"

What *was* he doing there sneaking around at night when all the stores were closed? More corporate espionage?

"I saw your helpers leave but not you, then I noticed the light was still on and the door was cracked open. I came to check that everything was all right."

A likely story. She crossed her arms. "Why were you at your shop so late? You aren't even open for business yet."

"I'm not," he admitted, a dimple winking into existence in his cheek. "But you aren't the only person who is preparing for a big event on Saturday. I was baking."

"Oh, right." Claire stood in the doorway, determined not to let him see the mess inside. The last thing she wanted was for her competitor to see that she had a plumbing problem.

"So, what's going on?"

Claire forced a smile. "Nothing. Just doing some baking, just like you."

Rob frowned, his eyes drifting down to her chest, where her soaking-wet shirt clung. His left brow quirked up. "You sure?"

Obviously Claire's claim of nothing being wrong while she was soaked wasn't going to pass muster with Mr. Prying Eyes. "Just a little problem with the bathroom sink."

Rob's gaze skirted over her shoulder toward the bathroom. "Anything I can help with?"

"No." Maybe he would use the fact that her bathroom was on the fritz against her. Could he call the town and have her shut down? Would he? The earnest look on his face indicated that he had noble intentions, but maybe he was a good actor.

There was another reason Claire didn't want to accept help. She didn't want to admit to anyone that she couldn't do this all herself, not after she'd fought so hard against Peter's constant insinuations that Sandcastles would never take off, that she couldn't make the bakery successful on her own. She didn't want Rob to think the only reason she could even stay open for the cupcake sale was because he had bailed her out. She didn't want anyone else to think that either. Most of all, she didn't want to think it herself.

"So you know how to fix plumbing?" The doubtful look on Rob's face only made Claire want to dig her heels in deeper.

"YouTube has all sorts of tutorial videos. I'll start there."

He must have seen the mulishness in her expression because he leaned forward and added, "I'm pretty good at fixing leaks. I'm not trying to sabotage you."

Claire hadn't even considered that he would make the problem worse. She bristled again. Although he had leaned closer by less than six inches, the air between them felt more intimate. Like they were companions, friends even.

"I'm sure you are, but I've fixed plenty of things in here, and I'm sure a little leak won't be my downfall." Claire frowned. Fixing a leak wasn't exactly like fixing a crack in the tile or a cabinet door. What if she tried to fix it and made it worse? "I don't want to impose on you. You have your own bakery to worry about."

Rob nodded, his gaze drifting back to the bathroom. "True. I'm sure you'll get this fixed in no time. But the truth is, I could use *your* help, and if you're busy fixing your bathroom, you might not be able to help me. What about a trade?"

Claire was about to turn back to her bathroom but paused, cocking her head. "A trade?"

"Yep. You'd be doing me a big favor."

Claire lifted her chin. "That depends on what the problem is."

His smile grew brighter than the overhead lights. "Ever since coming into your shop, I've been thinking about the cozy atmosphere you have going. I won't be able to put anything up before the grand opening, mind you, but I've been thinking that it might be nice to add some tables to the front of my store to invite customers to stay a while. The problem is, I have no idea how to do that. If you'll tell me where to start, I'll fix the leak in your sink. Sound fair?"

Claire pursed her lips and tapped her toe. She shouldn't barter with the competition who had moved in across the street. But without fixing that leak in her sink, she wouldn't be able to open her store come morning. And if she called Ralph, he would charge an arm and a leg, and there was no guarantee he was even available. What if he was out of town too?

"You have a deal." She held out her hand then gripped his firmly as he shook hers. She caught his eye. "But we fix the leak first."

He laughed. "You drive a hard bargain. Show me where the problem is."

❀

Rob had purposely worked late at his store that evening because he knew Claire would be baking her cupcakes at night after she closed. It was silly, he knew, but he'd been hoping to catch a glimpse of her, maybe even get up the nerve to suggest they grab something to eat.

From his shop, he could see the side of the building that housed Sandcastles. He'd seen her helpers leave one by one, but after several minutes, Claire hadn't come out. What was worse, the slice of light spilling out onto the alley told him that the door leading to the kitchen was ajar. Naturally, he'd gone over to investigate.

He didn't know what he'd expected, certainly not that he'd end up lying on his back on the damp, mopped-up floor of her bathroom trying to fix a leak in her plumbing. Luckily, the leak had been minor, and he'd fixed it the best he knew how.

It was a stroke of good luck, actually, and he hadn't been making up the part about wanting Claire's help. Okay, so he really hadn't planned on having a seating area over at Bradford Breads, but her café was cozy and inviting, and it wouldn't hurt to get her advice on how he could replicate that at his bakery. Besides, he knew she would never let him fix the leak if he didn't try to make it seem like an equal exchange.

Who knew? It could be a new beginning for them.

As he pulled out from under the sink, he stifled a groan. He wasn't young enough to lie on the floor on his back for that long anymore. He feigned a smile and stood, dusting off his knees. As he'd worked, Claire seemed to thaw toward him.

She returned his smile, but it was tentative. "Is it fixed?"

"Should be. Are you ready to give it a shot?"

She bit her lip and nodded. Although nervous, there was a hopeful gleam in her eye. He bent to open the shut-off valve, holding his breath as he turned the knob. The pipes pinged, but no water came gushing from the seams.

He turned to Claire and motioned to the faucet handles, confidence making the motion fluid. "Will you do the honors?"

A faint blush stained her cheeks as she stepped closer to him in the cramped bathroom. She smelled like vanilla. Hesitantly, she reached out to turn on the faucet. Water gushed into the sink. No drips. It looked as though his fix had worked.

When she turned to him, the relief was apparent in her face. Her eyes had warmed, softening toward him. "Thank you." She infused a world of gratitude into those two words.

He cleared his throat. "You're welcome."

She nodded. The color in her cheeks deepened as she turned away to shut off the taps. With her back still turned, she told him, "Come with me to the front of the store, and I'll give you some tips on how I set up the café."

As they passed the opening separating the kitchen from the café, Claire groped for the light switch. Several lights hanging from the high ceiling shed light on the empty space.

At night, with no one in the café but the two of them, the space seemed strangely empty, and the emptiness made it seem more intimate. Claire led him past the display case, dotted with the remnants of the day's baked goods, and toward the door.

She gestured to the front space. "What do you see?"

For some reason, he suspected it was a trick question. "Tables and chairs?"

"Good, but—" She walked forward, gesturing to the nearest table before turning to face him. "Don't look at them individually. Look at them as a whole. Do you see the way I've placed them?"

"Along the window?"

She gestured to the tables farther back from the window, closer to the display case and aisle where customers presumably ordered. "The ones at the window draw customers inside, but there's far too little space there. See how I've placed these tables diagonally from those along the window? It fills up the space but shouldn't cause a problem when customers pull out a chair or leave it there when they're finished. There's still a wide enough aisle to walk through. It's dark out, so you might not be able to see, but that's what I've done on the sidewalk as well."

"I remember." He hadn't thought anything of the checkerboard pattern of the tables then, but it seemed it had been deliberate. "That's your secret?"

She laughed. "Partly. The other part is to make the tables inviting. You see how each table has a succulent?"

"A what?"

"The plant. It's like a cactus, but these are less prickly. They don't need a lot of water or take up a lot of space, but they help to make the table inviting. It's more than a place to sit and eat. It's a place to do the daily crossword or chat with friends. Each table has a holder with folded napkins and a themed bowl for creamer that matches the sugar dish. Yes, I paid a little extra to buy so many with seashells on the side, but I think it adds its own charm to the tables."

"I don't remember seeing any of this outside."

Claire sighed. She rubbed the back of her neck. "It's true. The wind tends to blow away the napkins, and I learned the hard way that if I keep a small potted plant on the tables, customers will walk away with them. So the tables outside are somewhat plain. I try to liven it up during tourist season with some large pots of flowers in between the tables."

"I think you do a wonderful job."

She met his gaze for a moment, almost shy. Then she turned all business, straightening her spine as if she hadn't heard the compliment. "Is there anything else you need advice on?"

His smile turned chagrined. "It sounds as though I could use some decorating help. You've given me a lot to think about, though. After the grand opening, I'm going to give some thought to rearranging my store, but I don't want to have a café like you have. I can't compete with this, and why bother? If they want coffee, they can come over here, but I still want my place to look inviting like Sandcastles does."

The look in her eyes softened, and he knew he'd said the right thing. Truly, he didn't want to compete with her café. Ideas of how they could work together bubbled up, but he didn't voice them, sensing that might be pushing things too far.

"Are you hungry? I have plenty of pastry left over." Claire's voice was tentative, as if she expected him to say no. *As if.*

Rob tried to act nonchalant. "Yeah, I'd like that. I'm starving."

It took all of five minutes for Claire to choose some cupcakes from the case. She poured them each a coffee, carried it all on a tray to one of the tables, and gestured for him to sit. It still felt odd to be there after hours, but the cupcakes made it feel less like he was intruding.

Rob started in on his treat while Claire fiddled with the wrapper of hers. The cake was moist, the frosting creamy. "I can see why they're a hit around here. These are amazing."

Claire beamed as she pulled the wrapper from the cupcake. "Thank you."

He took another bite, stealing a moment to really look at her. It was hard not to compare her to the girl he'd met on the beach that one summer. She'd changed, but of course so had he. For some reason, he was still drawn to her. Maybe it was her inner sparkle, like she was enjoying life to the fullest. Or maybe it was the shy way she tucked her hair behind her ear, or the way her nose wrinkled when she smiled. He'd been drawn into her orbit from the second they'd first met.

"So tell me, what made you decide to open a bakery?" Had they been so similar, even back then?

She held a hand in front of her mouth for a moment more as she finished chewing. "I always loved baking, and it turns out I'm pretty good at it."

He winked. "No false modesty, I see."

Color flooded her cheeks, and she looked away, deeper into the store. She pointed at a display case. He followed the gesture to find an elaborate cake shaped like a sandcastle. The sides and turrets were dusted with something white and pink that couldn't possibly be sand, but from a distance, it had a similar appearance. The construction of the castle itself was no rudimentary boxed affair with crenellations. It had turrets and walls rising in tiers. It looked like something out of a historical film dusted in pink sugar.

"That's my specialty. What sets me apart. I used to make cakes like that for my daughter's birthday parties. She loved them, and so did her friends. I loved making them. Soon, neighbors were asking me to make cakes for them. When I got divorced, I needed to make a living." Claire gestured to the store. "And what better way than to do something I love?"

Rob heard the pride in her voice and turned his

attention back to her. "Wow, that's impressive. How old is your daughter?"

"Twenty-two. She's backpacking through Europe right now."

"She's adventurous." Even without Claire saying so, he could see that she was as proud of her daughter as she was the sandcastle cakes. The emotion was there, shining in her eyes.

Claire laughed. She shook her head, her lips tilting in an expression of chagrin. "She sure doesn't get it from me. I've barely left Lobster Bay my entire life."

"From where I'm sitting, Lobster Bay isn't a bad place to be."

A small furrow formed between her eyebrows as she studied him. After a moment, she took another bite of cupcake. "Why did you choose Lobster Bay for your store location? We don't have much to offer to draw in big chain stores."

Rob lifted one shoulder in a shrug. "Sentimentality, I guess. It's not a bad spot for a store. No other bakery specializing in bread is nearby. It's in the center of a chain of towns, and there is the flood of tourists every year. But mostly..." He turned his gaze to the window. The overhead light mirrored on the glass, throwing his reflection back at him. Beyond it, he could barely make out the shape of his shop. "I vacationed here when I was a teenager. I fell in love with it then. The last time was when I was fifteen." He turned his attention to her, catching her gaze with his. "I could have sworn that I remembered you from that time."

She shrugged. Rob searched her face for a sign that she really did remember him. He didn't see one, yet he was positive she was the girl he remembered. Apparently, he hadn't made a lasting impression.

"Why didn't you come back?" Claire's voice was soft, and she leaned slightly forward, as if weighing his answer.

"My mom got sick after that. Cancer."

"I'm so sorry." She lifted her hand, almost as if she meant to comfort him. He wished she would touch him, breach that gap between them, but her hand fell back to her coffee mug, and she took a sip.

He nodded solemnly, accepting her condolences. He'd gotten good at that. "After she died, I guess I just went through all the motions like I thought I should. I went to college and got a business degree. I started baking bread after I graduated. My mom always baked bread, and I guess it was familiar and comforting. I turned it into a job. I met the love of my life, got married, and then she…"

"You don't have to talk about that," Claire said in a rush. She looked horrified.

"No, it's okay. That was a while ago, and it's not so painful anymore." He looked up at her, pinning her hazel eyes with his gaze. "Truth is I'm ready to move on, make a new start. That's why I chose Lobster Bay for my store."

Claire's eyes widened, and she looked away, but before she did, he saw a little spark. Was it a spark of interest? Or sympathy for his wife's death? Rob couldn't tell. At the very least, he felt he had removed some of her suspicion about his reason for coming there. Maybe now was a good time to ask about working together again.

He finished the cupcake in front of him as he practiced the words in his head.

"Your sale on Saturday will go off without a hitch. You bake fantastic cupcakes. I'm sure your customers will be begging for more."

Pink tinged her cheeks, and her smile was bright. "Thank you."

He leaned forward. "I think you can do even better if we take advantage of our shops being across the street to capitalize on your sale and my grand opening. It will get us both customers."

A hint of wariness entered her gaze. "How?"

"For one thing, we could set up a small table at each other's store. A tabletop sign or some flyers with the details, a few bite-sized free samples. I would cut some bread into cubes and put them out with cheese dip. If you made a batch of mini cupcakes or even cut up some of the larger ones into quarters, it could serve the same purpose. We'll drive customers across the street. Because it isn't far, I'm sure we'll get a lot of foot traffic that way."

For a moment, Claire didn't say anything. Her mouth was pursed. She was clearly thinking hard.

He counted that moment as a triumph. If she wasn't dismissing the idea right off the bat, he was starting to get through to her. The evidence of progress made his heart sing. He didn't mind putting in a little extra effort for Claire.

"I'll think about it."

"Good. Can I help you clean up?" He picked up his plate and mug, then stood, the chair scraping back on the floor.

"Oh, no. It will only take me a second." She took the plate and mug from him.

"Okay then. Thanks for the snack." He started toward the back door then turned. "Let me know what you decide either way. I promise you, I only want what's best—for both of us."

Words would only take him so far. He didn't want to overstay his welcome and give her a chance to distrust him. He bid her goodnight and left. He didn't want to leave. He could have stayed up all night talking to her. There were still so many things about her that he didn't know, so many things about his life he wanted to share. But all of that would come in time, if he had his way.

He hadn't become the owner of a successful business with multiple locations by giving up at the first sign of trouble. He wasn't going to quit now, not when he was just starting down the path to his well-earned new beginning.

This time, he was going to get things right.

CHAPTER EIGHTEEN

Claire completed her morning routine on autopilot. Her body was there, petting and feeding Urchin, getting ready for work, but her mind remained on Rob's proposal. Work together. Could they?

Had she gotten him all wrong, jumped to conclusions about his intentions with setting up a bakery across the street from hers? Sandcastles was a symbol of her success, a part of her, but was she too close to her business to think straight? Jane and Maxi certainly thought so, and they'd never steered her wrong before.

And then there was the attraction. Rob certainly was easy on the eyes, and working with him wouldn't be a hardship. Though, Claire didn't want to take things any further than business. Peter's betrayal still stung, and she didn't want to open herself up to that again.

Claire felt a pang of guilt for not admitting to Rob she indeed remembered him from fifteen years ago. At first, she'd been afraid it would give him the upper hand to know she recalled that night, and her ego had been bruised. He hadn't bothered to contact her.

Now that she knew about his mom getting sick, it made sense that he never returned. He had more important things to deal with than finding a girl he kissed once in the moonlight.

Claire was feeling pretty positive when she finally settled onto her Vespa and cranked the key. But as the engine purred to life, doubts crept into her thoughts. Why was he working so late at his bakery? He'd said he was baking bread, but why couldn't he get that done during the day? It wasn't like he had to wait on customers like she did. He wasn't open yet. Maybe he preferred to bake at night.

But he'd fixed her pipes, which enabled her to stay open. If he really wanted her to fail, wouldn't he have just claimed he didn't know anything about plumbing? Claire didn't know if she was being overly suspicious. She needed advice before she made any decisions about teaming up with Bradford Breads. Would that be a good marketing move, or would it be a mistake?

Luckily, Claire had an expert in marketing at her fingertips. Tammi. Claire would call her as soon as she reached the shop.

Doubts tickled her stomach in the predawn light as she drove to the store. The gray sky was starting to lighten when she parked her Vespa and walked the short distance to her bakery. In the early morning, before anyone else was out, she could hear the ocean waves and smell the sea. As she was about to unlock the door, movement across the street caught her eye. Rob. Claire stopped short, her key halfway to the lock on the front door. Doubts warred with a warm, fuzzy feeling in her stomach. It swarmed like butterflies taking flight as their eyes met across the street.

He lifted his hand in greeting. With nervous electricity zinging through her, she did the same. As he disappeared inside his store, she turned her back to enter hers.

Although the shop was dark and empty, the quiet reminded her of their evening together the night before, filling in some of the blanks in their lives since they'd first met. Of the way he'd fixed the leak in her pipe. And that friendly wave that, for some reason, filled her with energy.

As she stepped into the kitchen and groped for the lights, she fiddled with the zipper on her purse, in search of her phone. Hopefully Tammi would answer and be able to talk.

As the phone rang, garbled in her ear, Claire crossed to the table in the kitchen and dropped the oversized tote bag she carried onto it. She took stock of the kitchen.

Everything was neat and tidy, exactly as she had left it. She had muffins to bake this morning as well as croissants to finish and put in the display case.

"Hello? Mom?"

Claire smiled at her daughter's voice. The quality of the call was a bit tinny, but warmth bloomed in her chest even so. When Tammi had gone to college, Claire had gotten used to not seeing her every day, but it was still hard. She never felt she had enough time for Tammi when her daughter came home.

"Hi, honey. Do you have a minute? I could use some advice."

"Advice?" Tammi sounded instantly more alert, maybe even excited.

"I told you about the bakery going up across the street, didn't I?"

"Yes…"

"Well, the owner came in to talk to me. We're both having sales tomorrow. His is a two-for-one on bread, and mine is buy one cupcake, get two free. He said he wants to work together to send customers across the street to each other's stores."

"Oh! Cross-promotion." Although she didn't say as much outright, Tammi sounded approving. A note of hesitation crept into her voice as she asked, "Does he sell cupcakes too?"

"No, his store strictly sells bread."

"Well then, I don't see how you have anything to lose. What sort of cross-promotion did he have in mind?"

Claire leaned her hip against the counter, her mind returning to that late-night conversation. "He wants to set up a table in each other's stores with free samples and flyers pointing to the sale."

"That sounds like a great idea! Nothing like a free sample to get people to try out your goods, and you make great cupcakes, Mom. I'm sure you'll have customers stampeding across the street to take you up on the sale."

Claire laughed at that image. Her daughter had been the eternal optimist and her biggest cheerleader ever since Claire had opened her bakery in the charming, old building. "I don't know about that. But you think I should take him up on the offer?"

"Yeah. It sounds like it would cost you nothing and gain you a lot. Do it!"

A knot of tension unwound from between Claire's shoulders at the cut-and-dried answer. Now she didn't have to keep wallowing in indecision. Tammi knew more about marketing and promotion than Claire did. If her daughter said to do it, then she would do exactly that.

"Thanks, baby. I don't want to keep you from your vacation."

"Love you, Mom."

"Love you too."

Claire's chest ached a bit as she hung up the phone. The sooner her daughter returned from Europe, the better. As much as Claire knew she was having fun and experiencing something that most people never got to, she couldn't help but worry. Although, ever since Claire had decided to have the cupcake sale, she'd been too busy with preparations to worry. She didn't know whether or not that was a good thing.

Hailey wasn't scheduled to come in until later, which meant Claire had extra work to do, so she tried to put it out of her mind as she prepared for the day. After she had the muffins baking in the oven and the croissant dough arranged on a cookie sheet, ready to go in next, she went to the front of the store. The sun had come up, beaming down out of a sky dotted with wispy clouds. As she went about the business of opening up, her eye was drawn to the bakery across the street. Rob must have gotten new blinds, and they were down across all the windows, so no one could see inside.

She wasn't hoping to see *him*, of course, but she was curious if he would rearrange things based on her advice. Perhaps he needed help setting up. If she was going to team up with him to cross-promote during the sale, she would need to bring over a few things anyway, including the cupcake samples. She needed to frost those first and make a space for his samples in her shop.

She pulled two tables together along the wall next to the sugar and milk station, removing the chairs. A table alone wasn't enough of a draw. She needed to do something to make it look homier.

The timer on her phone beeped, and she hurried into the back to remove the muffins and get the croissants baking. Then she rooted around the kitchen, searching out everything she had that she was not already using. She found three wicker baskets and a crisp white tablecloth to arrange on the tables and set them aside. By the time she filled the display case with the baked goods she'd made that morning, still warm from the oven, it was time to open the store.

Bert and Harry waited outside her door with broad smiles and cheery waves. She answered them, her gaze slipping past to Bradford Breads. The bakery still showed no signs of life.

She opened the door and shooed the two old men inside. "Go ahead and sit at your table. I'll bring you the usual."

"You're a doll," Harry said with a fond smile.

Within minutes, she had set them up with steaming cups of coffee and warm blueberry muffins at their usual table.

"How goes the cupcake preparations?" asked Bert.

"Very well," Claire responded, relieved not to have to lie on that front. After last night, she had baked the last of the cupcakes she would need to make. Tonight would come the colossal task of frosting them all.

"Are you going to give us a hint at the flavors you'll be having? I need to prepare myself for how many I'll be taking home."

Claire laughed at Bert's question. "The usual chocolate and vanilla, plus red velvet, chocolate mocha, lemon raspberry and the others I'll leave as a surprise. If you come to the sale I'll set aside some samples," she said with a wink. "I promise you'll be pleased."

Another customer entered, someone Claire didn't recognize—a tourist. She hurried over to serve them. Hailey would arrive any minute for her shift, but in the meantime, Claire was consumed with serving her customers. By the time her help came in, Claire was relieved. She handed over the front of the shop to Hailey and retreated into the back to fetch the baskets.

When she brought them to the table, she was satisfied to note that the tables inside and outside were cluttered with customers. More took their coffee to go in paper cups and carried out paper bags with their purchased baked goods. A thrill of gratification buzzed through her as she noticed early-morning tourists pausing to look at the sandwich board Hailey had set up outside announcing her sale. Everything was finally coming together.

Humming cheerfully under her breath, Claire arranged the baskets on the table invitingly. She left space for the flyers Rob had mentioned advertising his sale. With the free samples of his bread in the basket, and the bright red of his sale flyers she saw around town, customers would flock to that corner after purchasing their cupcakes at the counter. Thinking about the flyers reminded her that she still needed to give some of hers to Jane. Stacy had dropped them off, and they were in the kitchen. She could give them to Jane tonight when she came over to frost unless she got a chance to drop them off earlier today.

"What's all that about?" Harry gestured to the display at the nearest table.

Bert lowered his newspaper with bald curiosity.

Claire smiled. "It's a surprise. You'll have to wait to find out."

The old men chuckled. Harry said, "You sure are keeping the mystery about yourself today. You know how to string an old man along."

Claire winked. "And hopefully the rest of the town too."

"Oh, I'm sure you'll get a fair few in here tomorrow. The only question is if we can get here early enough to claim our table!"

Claire wanted to promise to save it for them—after all, it was regulars like Bert and Harry who kept her afloat when the tourists left. However, at that moment, the bell over the door chimed, and Claire looked up.

Her stomach sank like a stone as first Sandee then Claire's ex-husband stepped into the shop. Leave it to them to ruin a happy morning simply by showing up. Maybe they would just make their purchase quickly and leave. Too bad she couldn't sneak out back and have Hailey wait on them. She would have to walk right past them to get to the kitchen.

Claire plastered a smile on her face. "Good morning."

She didn't see Peter often since the divorce, thankfully. Tammi had just graduated high school when it happened, so she was old enough to visit her father on her own. Claire's stomach still tightened a little whenever she saw him, like she was waiting for the next nasty thing he would say. But that was simple self-preservation. She knew him well enough. He might have a new, younger wife, but Sandee hadn't sweetened his disposition.

He grunted and jerked his chin at the store across the street. "The new bread place isn't open yet? I was hoping to stop in there."

Claire held her smile in place through will alone. If there was one silver lining, it was that the years hadn't been kind to him since they'd parted. His hairline had receded almost to the crown of his head. His comb-over was doing a poor job of hiding that. The fact that she had ever loved him was a mystery to her. How had she not seen through his bullshit?

"He's not opening until Saturday. Maybe you should come back then."

Peter swung his gaze to meet hers again. "You don't seem worried about a bakery going in across the street."

"I'm not," she said, biting off her words. "He only offers bread. I offer so much more."

Peter raised his eyebrows. "I'm sure that nice little bakery in Bar Harbor offered much more than bread too. That didn't stop Bradford Breads from putting them out of business last summer. Right in the middle of tourist season."

Claire frowned. Was that true? Would that happen to her? No, she had her cupcake sale, and she and Rob were working together. This was just the sort of thing Peter would make up to upset her. Well, it wasn't going to work this time.

Sandee, turned away and tapping her chin with a long, ruby-colored fake nail as she peered through the glass at the baked goods on display, chimed in absently, "I heard that owner in Bar Harbor didn't see it coming. I guess the Bradford Breads owner was as sweet as pie to him." She straightened, gestured at the chocolate croissants, and held up two fingers to Hailey, who had just come out from the kitchen.

Claire didn't say a word. They were only trying to get under her skin.

With a bright smile, Sandee settled into the crook of Peter's arm. "If you ask me, I think the owner probably acts nice while he puzzles out what makes a bakery so successful. Then he emulates it and cuts into their business by doing more advertising. He can afford it with a big chain like that."

Claire swallowed hard, trying to keep her expression confident. She was afraid she failed miserably.

Fortunately, Sandee and Peter weren't looking at

her. They were too preoccupied, staring across the street.

Sandee mused, "I have to admit, it's brilliant the way he's got the shades down. It really makes you wonder what it looks like inside." She turned and leaned forward, delicately glossing her fingers over Claire's shoulder. "Not that it will be able to compete with Sandcastles. You have a knack for decorating. I'm sure nothing Bradford Breads can come up with will compare."

"Thank you," Claire muttered, but it was through gritted teeth and a forced smile.

Had she handed her best decorating tips directly into the hands of the enemy?

"Your croissants?" Hailey prompted from behind the counter. Judging by the look on her face, she didn't approve of the way the conversation was going. Claire imagined she was trying to push Sandee and Peter out of the store as quickly as possible. Sandee tugged Peter toward the register to pay for them, buying Claire some time to compose herself.

She found herself staring at the shaded windows of the shop across the street and kicking herself. Had she fallen for the exact game that Sandee and Peter had warned her about? Rob had been nice to her, had helped her, and now his windows were shaded, and he might be rearranging his shop last-minute to draw her customers away. Why hadn't she known about Bar Harbor? Why hadn't she done more research before she trusted the owner of a rival bakery?

The fact that her ex-husband and his wife were the ones to throw this in her face was adding insult to injury. Sick to her stomach, Claire tore herself away from the sight of the other shop.

See what happens when you try to be nice? When you trust others? She should have learned her lesson from her marriage. She stormed over and ripped apart the display she'd put together, returning the two tables to the way they had been previously.

How stupid could she be, agreeing to work with a man who was going to undermine her and put her out of business?

She tucked the wicker baskets under her arm and was about to stow them back in the kitchen when a tourist emerged from the washroom. He searched the shop, and upon seeing her fiddling with the chairs, he made a beeline for her. She straightened, ready to greet the customer despite how drained she was.

"Uh, ma'am? The water pressure in the bathroom is a little low. I thought you'd want to know."

She pressed her lips together as her heart raced. She

set the wicker baskets on top of the display case. *Calm, slow movements.* She wasn't panicking.

How could the water pressure be low? They repaired the pipes last night. Her eyes flicked to the store across the street. Had Rob really fixed them, or had he done something to sabotage her so she wouldn't be open tomorrow for the cupcake sale?

Claire was tense as she slipped into the public washroom and turned on the tap. Water poured out in a slow stream, but it appeared to be working. The toilet flushed, taking a long time to fill up again. She checked under the sink for a leak but found none. Everything *seemed* to be okay, but did the low water pressure indicate some catastrophe was lurking?

Maybe she should call Sally, just in case.

CHAPTER NINETEEN

*J*ane had a thousand and one things to do to keep the inn running smoothly, but most of her time was spent checking that her mother hadn't removed her slippers and bandages. Her feet were still raw and cut up from her escapade on the beach, and her nurse friend had said they would be for another week at least. She would have thought that would keep Addie out of trouble because it made her less likely to walk away.

Not so.

It was only just after noon, but Addie was sleeping now, curled up on her bed with a blanket thrown over her shoulders and her feet peeking out from the bottom edge. The slippers were still on, and the socks and bandages underneath. She looked so peaceful while asleep, even though the lines etched into her face had appeared to deepen over the span of just a few months. She was aging so fast, right in front of Jane, and she didn't know what to do. She loved her mother. All she wanted was to keep her safe and happy.

But doing this, running after Addie to make sure she was still in the inn or hadn't left a dangerous appliance running or kicked off her shoes, made Jane feel like the mother rather than the child.

Softly, she closed the door and sighed. What was she going to do?

She wasn't about to ask her sister for help. Andie had left after high school and seemingly didn't care what happened back in Lobster Bay. Sure, she'd tried to be a comfort when Jane's son had died, and again when her husband, Brad, had died. But Jane could always tell that Andie couldn't wait to get back to her fancy life in New York City. She'd kept Andie apprised of their mother's condition but had glossed over how bad it was. What would be the point of going into details?

She retreated back downstairs to the lobby, where she'd taken out the ledger. A family was due to check out of the inn today, and an older woman, Mrs. Weatherlee, who used to live in town ages ago, wanted a reservation in a few weeks. At least they had a few reservations. Bookings had dropped off that summer, and Jane had no idea why. Perhaps word had gotten out that the innkeeper's daughter didn't know what she was doing.

Jane went to the foyer, where she'd put the ledger books to work on while she watched the inn. At least her accounting background helped with the financial aspect of running Tides. Numbers were what she knew best. Numbers were soothing. Numbers always made sense.

Unless they were scratched in her mother's handwriting.

As a headache built behind her eyes, Jane scrunched up her nose and saught the exact sum on the chart that had turned the numbers so awry.

The door opened, letting in a burst of salty air and a broad-shouldered male form. Jane glanced up, smiling despite her weariness. It deepened when she saw that the newcomer was not a customer but Rob Bradford.

"Good morning."

He smiled and held up a sheaf of papers. "Good morning. I brought the information I have on memory care facilities. I visited a lot of these in person before, to look around. Would you like to go through them together?"

Jane's shoulders rounded inward. She didn't want to

have to face this alone. Maybe she *should* wait for her sister. But no, Andie probably wouldn't stay long enough to sort any of it out, and besides, Jane wasn't sure she even wanted her sister's input with something that important.

Rob couldn't help her make her decision, but he could give her the information she needed. She nodded and slipped off the stool behind the rustic counter they used as a check-in desk. She slid the ledger out of sight and beckoned him toward the kitchen. "That would be nice. Come, I'll make you a cup of coffee."

Once they were ensconced at the table, steaming mugs between their hands and the papers spread out before them, Rob looked around. "No muffins today?"

"I haven't gone down to Claire's bakery in a few days. I take it she's very busy preparing for the sale tomorrow. How are your preparations going for your grand opening?"

"Very well," he said with a smile. "I think—I *hope* —Claire and I will be working together to cross-promote. I spoke with her yesterday about setting up a table in each other's stores, and I think she might be coming around."

Jane was surprised. So, Claire had finally come to her senses. Good. "That's great to hear. I hope all three of our businesses can work together in the near future."

He raised his mug to her. "That is my plan, as long as Claire is amenable to it as well." He sipped, pausing. "Unless she said something different to you?" He asked casually, but there was something about the way he didn't meet her gaze that hinted the question was weighing on his mind.

"I'm sorry, I haven't spoken to her recently. Is something worrying you?"

He took another sip to cover his reaction, but Jane noticed the color tinging his cheeks. "No, it's just— well, we didn't actually make the final plans. I'm hoping she'll come to me."

Jane could tell that he liked Claire, not only liked her as a person but was attracted to her. And from the way Jane had witnessed her friend behave around the mere mention of Rob, she was almost certain that the attraction went both ways. There was something familiar, comforting, about Rob that Jane couldn't put her finger on. It wasn't only the kind way he'd treated her mother or how he'd rescued Addie from the storm. It was him. After the way Peter had treated Claire, Rob would be a refreshing change.

He was a good man with a good heart. He'd gone to all this trouble to help Jane with Addie. She looked down at the myriad pamphlets and notes strewn between them. Immediately, she felt out of her depth, like a fish out of water. She was far more comfortable thinking about Claire's love life.

Taking a deep breath, she squared her shoulders and looked Rob in the eye. "Okay. Tell me what you know about these facilities."

❦

More than an hour later, Rob left, and Jane was still conflicted. Her head swam with all the new information. If she put Addie in a memory care facility, she had three top contenders to choose from. All had professional, caring, patient staffs and were close by.

But as clear-cut as all that data was, Jane was still struggling. In more lucid days, Addie had mentioned she never wanted to go to a facility. But she'd been referring to a nursing home, one where the patients were lined up in beds and neglected.

These places that Rob had shown her were more like residences. Rob assured her it was like having a room in her own home. The staff was lovely, the food good. Jane didn't want to betray her mother, but she felt like a ghost of herself trying to look after Addie and run the inn at the same time. She didn't know what to do. She needed advice. Luckily tonight was the night she'd promised to help Claire frost the cupcakes for her sale. She would get all the advice she needed from Claire and Maxi.

CHAPTER TWENTY

*T*he shop Rob had leased in Lobster Bay was small. In any other location, he would have set up aisles to stock as much bread on the shelves as possible. However, he didn't want Claire to think he was ungrateful for her advice or that he'd only concocted it as an excuse to spend time with her.

So instead of baking more bread for his shelves, he pulled down the window blinds so no one could see what he was doing and spent the day rearranging the store to accommodate a cozy cluster of tables near the door.

Across from those, in the most prominent spot in the store, he arranged a table with paper wrappers ready to be filled with cupcake samples. He even made a sign with her bakery name to pin to the front of the table with the location of those delicious cupcakes. All that was left was for her to add the product and any promotional materials she had about the cupcake sale. Since Claire couldn't see inside with the shades drawn, he hoped it would be a pleasant surprise.

All day, he waited for her to march over and agree to his bargain, but she never came. When her store was about to close and she still hadn't made her way across the street, despite seeing her look his way several times in the distance, he decided to bite the bullet. He'd gone through all that trouble to accommodate her store. Surely it wouldn't be *too* untoward of him to ask her to take a look.

Yes, she would probably want to see it. And besides, they should talk about any strategy they might want to use to draw in more customers and send them to each other's stores.

Decided, Rob locked up his store and crossed the street, empty of tourists at this hour. Claire was clearly getting ready to close. She'd already pulled her sandwich board inside the shop and was wiping down the tables. He reached for the door latch, hoping that he wouldn't find it locked.

A bell tinkled overhead as he stepped into her bakery. It smelled sweet, chocolate and vanilla scenting the air and making his mouth water.

At the noise, Claire raised her head with a cheerful smile. It faded the moment she saw him. The disappearance was like a punch to the gut.

"I was just closing up."

The formal words were spoken in the frostiest tone he'd ever heard. She had been so open and friendly with him last night. What had changed?

"I don't want to keep you from your work, but you hadn't gotten back to me regarding our joint promotion. I set up a table, and I thought—"

Claire scrubbed at the table, barely giving him a glance. "Oh, sorry. I got to thinking maybe that wasn't the best idea."

"Really? Why?" Last night she seemed receptive. What happened to change her mind?

When she turned to face him, her expression was conflicted. Her face was stony, but her eyes flickered with indecision. They stared at each other for a few seconds, then she lifted her chin, defiant. She looked away, focusing on wiping down the already spotless table. "I just feel it might not be in my best interest."

"I don't see why not. I mean, our products complement each other's, and we're both having a sale—"

She turned from her task, crossing her arms over her chest. "I'm not interested right now. Maybe next time.

But now, I have dozens of cupcakes to frost, so if you don't mind, I'd like to close up."

He met her gaze, trying to read the truth in her eyes. This was not the friendly woman he'd had cupcakes with last night. Had he done something to offend her? Or had last night been the aberration, when she was caught off her guard due to her crisis. He sensed there was no more to say. Claire had apparently made up her mind.

"Okay, well, good luck tomorrow, then." He left, disappointed and more than a little disheartened.

CHAPTER TWENTY-ONE

"What was that all about?" Hailey stood in the doorway that led to the kitchen, the keys to her grandfather's car dangling from her hand. She hadn't been eavesdropping, not exactly. She just hadn't wanted to interrupt what seemed like a very intense conversation.

Claire glanced out the window, a look of regret passing across her face. "That was the owner of Bradford Breads. He wanted to combine forces for the sale."

"And you think that's a bad idea?" Hailey had heard enough to know the man sounded sincere whereas Claire had been standoffish, almost rude. "It sounded like you guys had an arrangement worked out prior."

Claire sighed and returned to wiping the table quite vigorously. "I didn't get a chance to tell you, but he came over last night and fixed the pipe in the bathroom. It sprung a leak."

Hailey frowned. That didn't sound like something a competitor would do. "So it turns out he's a nice guy, then."

Claire straightened and folded the cloth into a neat square. "Well, he seemed nice last night."

Hailey felt relieved. If the bread store didn't want to put them out of business, then that made her job more secure and perhaps opened the opportunity for more responsibility and more pay. "Then maybe working with him would increase business. Why did you say no?"

"I found out that he puts people out of business. I think he was sneaking around, trying to find out things to use against us." Claire went over to lock the door, pausing to look out across the street.

Hailey wasn't so sure about the motivation being to get information. What kind of information could he possibly get that would hurt them? From what she'd overheard, the Bradford guy was clearly disappointed they wouldn't team up, and Hailey sensed something else too. The man was interested in more than just a business relationship. He was interested in Claire. Couldn't she see that? Or was rejecting his business proposal a way for her to keep anyone from getting around the wall she'd built around her heart after her divorce?

Judging by the regretful look on her face, Claire might feel the same way about him.

"Anyway, it's not going to happen now. We'll see what happens in the future." Claire turned from the door and headed to the kitchen. "Aren't you supposed to be taking off? Oh, that reminds me. I saw that you were driving some old beater the other night. Is something wrong with your car? If you need money for it, I can give you a loan or maybe a bonus if we make a lot on the cupcake sale."

Hailey was horrified. Her pride would never let her take a handout, especially not from Claire, who had been so good to her already. "Oh, no! Frank just had to —umm—wait for a part. Mine will be fixed soon. Don't worry."

Claire looked at her a bit too long, and Hailey almost confessed, but then Claire nodded. "Okay great."

Hailey walked with her back to the kitchen. "I put out all the ingredients for you. Have fun tonight. I wish I could help."

"No worries. We'll be up past Jennifer's bedtime, and I have plenty of help with Jane and Maxi. I need you rested for tomorrow. It's going to be a big day."

Claire left the side door unlocked. Jane and Maxi would be there any minute, so she took out the big mixing bowls, spatulas, and frosting bags and set them next to the ingredients that Hailey had taken out. The flyers she'd had printed sat in the corner. Claire had already posted some around town, but she'd set a few aside for Jane, as she hadn't had a chance to get them to her yet.

She'd already put several dozen cupcakes out of their containers to let them get to room temperature, and she lined them up on the table in front of the chairs, then started on the frosting. She made three bowls, a lemon flavor, a vanilla, and a mocha.

"Jane Miller reporting for duty." Jane peeked her head in the door, holding up a brown bag. "I brought you a sandwich compliments of Brenda."

"Thank you." Come to think of it, Claire hadn't eaten. She took the bag and opened it. "Ham and swiss? My favorite. You want half?"

Jane shook her head. "I ate at the inn."

"Knock, knock." Maxi opened the screen door, careful to latch it behind her. "I brought you a salad."

"Thanks." Claire's answer was muffled since her mouth was full of sandwich.

"Oh, I see you're already eating." Maxi smiled at Jane. "Great minds think alike."

"I appreciate them both." Claire put the salad on the table and took another bite of the sandwich. While still chewing, she grabbed the bowls of frosting and set them on the table next to their respective cupcakes. "Okay, I figure we can each take a flavor. Maxi you get lemon raspberry, Jane you can do the red velvet, and I'll do the chocolate mocha. I use a pastry bag so that the frosting is a big thick swirl."

Claire loaded her bag and demonstrated how to frost the cupcakes, twirling the bag so the frosting spiraled up in a thick swirl then pulling the top to a peak. "Got it?"

"Yep."

Claire watched them focus intently on the task. Jane was more meticulous, calculating the swirl so that it was precisely even. Maxi more creative. Claire started in on her own.

"I passed Hailey on the way down here. She's still driving that car," Maxi said.

"I asked her about it." Claire set her cupcake down and picked up the next. "She's just waiting for hers to be fixed."

"That's not what Frank told me." Jane looked at Claire over the top of her cupcake. "He said her car needed a lot of work, and she can't afford it. That's her grandfather's car she's driving now."

Claire frowned. "Why would she tell me that she was just waiting for Frank to fix it?"

"Pride. And maybe she didn't want to worry you with all this going on." Maxi gestured to the cupcakes spread out on the table.

Worry bloomed in Claire's gut. If Hailey was concerned, did that mean she thought Sandcastles might lose business? For Claire to worry was one thing, but if others did too…

"Well, nothing to worry about at all now that you're teaming up with Bradford Breads. That must be a relief," Jane said.

Claire's fist tightened, and frosting surged out of the bag in an unsightly blob. "Where did you hear that?"

She put the unsalvageable cupcake down on the table. *Great, one less piece of inventory for the sale.*

The messy frosting blob didn't seem to bother Maxi though. She pulled it in front of her and started peeling off the paper wrapper. "We get to eat the mistakes, right?"

"Yes, eat the mistakes," Claire said to Maxi, but her eyes were on Jane, who now looked confused.

"Rob told me. He came over to Tides earlier."

Interesting, now why would he do that if he wasn't

supplying them with bread? Claire's gaze fell on the flyers. *Aha!* He'd probably brought her a flyer for his shop, likely trying to get his posted in front of Claire's.

Claire grabbed the flyers from the counter and handed them to Jane. "Here are those flyers. I suppose you already put the one for Bradford Breads up."

Jane frowned. "Huh?"

"You said Rob was at Tides…"

"He had promised to bring the pamphlets on the memory care facilities the other day, so he was dropping them off. He didn't bring any flyers though." Jane took the flyers from Claire.

"And he said we were working together?" How presumptuous. Claire specifically remembered saying she would think about it before she'd turned him down outright earlier in the day. He must have visited Tides before that.

Jane scrunched her nose. "No, not exactly. He said that he'd offered and you seemed as though you were coming around to the idea."

Claire crossed her arms. "Well, I'm not."

"Why not?"

"I'm just not sure about him."

Jane's eyes softened, the crease between her eyebrows gone. "Well, I am. He's a good man. He didn't have to do all the kind things he's done for me and my mother, but he has."

He might seem nice to Jane, but she didn't know how he made a habit of putting bakeries out of business. "Peter and Sandee came into the shop earlier. They told me about a bakery he put out of business in Bar Harbor. He acts nice then steals the very things that make a bakery successful, implements them, and out-advertises them until they can't afford to compete anymore. I won't fall into his trap."

Maxi scoffed. She had frosting on her nose from eating Claire's cupcake mistake, so it was a little hard to take her seriously. "Claire, consider the source. When has Sandee or Peter ever done a thing to help you? I bet they'd say anything just to chip at your confidence, including driving a wedge into what sounds like a good business decision."

"You say that, but…" Claire hesitated. Maxi had a point, and last night Rob had seemed so sincere, not to mention that Tammi thought teaming up was a good idea. But then there was the water pressure issue.

"But what?" Maxi asked.

Claire stifled a sigh. She studied the horizon as she recounted what had happened last night. "I was at the store late, and one of my pipes started leaking. I wouldn't be able to open the store without fixing it, and

Sally was out of town. Rob showed up practically out of nowhere. He said he was working late too." She turned, picked up another cupcake, and started to apply the frosting. "He fixed the pipe, and I thought everything was fine, but now the water pressure is lower than it was this morning. What if he did something to the pipes to put me out of commission tomorrow? It's not as though I have enough experience to tell either way."

"Impossible," Jane pronounced. "I don't think he could do something to the water pressure from the bathroom sink. That would only affect that sink. You'd have to do something to the main line. And anyway, Rob isn't that sort of man."

"Weren't you just complaining that the pipes are on their way out?" Maxi asked. "I'm sure you mentioned something about it and the cost it would be to fix them. Ralph told you they had to be replaced, didn't he? I don't think it's right to assume Rob did something."

"Yes," Claire admitted begrudgingly. She sighed and rubbed her forehead. What if she had made the wrong call in not teaming up with Rob? When she'd told him she'd changed her mind, he hadn't acted angry or smug like she'd thought a competitor trying to sabotage her might act. He'd acted hurt. "I suppose you're right. It's not fair to make assumptions about Rob, but I still think I'm better off running the sale on my own."

A deep groan sounded from the pipes, as if the very building disagreed, and they all looked at the ceiling. They went back to frosting their cupcakes. It was time for a change of topic.

"So did you find any facilities you liked? Are you really considering that?" Claire asked.

Jane's expression turned grim. "I'm afraid I might have to. I'm finding it so hard to care for her and run the inn. Both are full-time jobs, and I'm stretched so thin."

Claire had been careful about the advice she'd given Jane on the subject. She knew it was too much for one person to handle, but never being in that position herself, she didn't want to push Jane into anything she wasn't comfortable with. Jane was coming to the same conclusion on her own, and Claire was there to support her.

"I don't know how much longer I can do this, but it feels so awful to put Mom into a facility," Jane echoed.

"We know you want what's best for her," Claire said.

Maxi piped up. "And her well-being is important. This is about her health. If she's going to hurt herself without meaning to, she needs help."

With a heavy sigh, Jane brushed a short strand of hair out of her face. "I know that. But I feel like a terrible daughter for wanting to make her somebody else's problem. I feel like I should be trying harder."

"That's not fair on you. You can't do everything yourself," Maxi answered.

Claire understood her friend's thought process far better. It was difficult to trust someone, difficult to hand over work that she could be doing better herself. She was learning that this week too. Although a small voice in her mind still whispered that she would be able to bake and frost all these cupcakes better, she couldn't do it as fast. She had made a sacrifice.

Maybe Jane needed to make a sacrifice too.

"I think you should really consider the way it would lighten the burden if Addie was taken care of by professionals. I know it isn't what she wants, but she isn't of sound mind, or you wouldn't be in this situation."

Every other time Claire had made the suggestion, Jane had dismissed it. Sometimes casually, sometimes with more heat. Today, she only nodded wearily. "I know. I am considering it. Rob stopped by today with some pamphlets and other information and walked me through the best choices for her. I know it's the right thing to do, but there's something inside me that just feels like a failure."

In a small voice, Maxi asked, "Wouldn't you feel like a failure if she hurt herself badly? If she had to go to the hospital or even died because she wasn't able to care for herself the way she used to and you were stretched too thin to do it yourself?"

Jane nodded. "You're right. I would. So you guys don't think I'm being selfish?"

Claire's brows shot up. "Selfish? You're anything but. You've given up your retirement to run Tides the way your mom wants and take care of her. It's not selfish to put her in a place where she'll be safe and well cared for. If you continue the way you are, you'll probably burnout and not be able to do either job."

"Claire's right," Maxi said. "And remember, no matter what you decide, we're behind you one hundred percent."

Claire nodded her agreement. If anyone was selfish, it was Claire. Maxi and Jane didn't think Bradford Breads was a threat, and she valued their opinions very much. Yet there she was, worrying over the store across the street when Jane had real issues to deal with. Claire picked up the next cupcake, determined to think things through more objectively just as soon as the big sale was over tomorrow.

CHAPTER TWENTY-TWO

C laire woke to sharp pinpricks of pain on her
scalp. She winced, swatting at the offender.
Her fingers met soft fur as Urchin climbed off her head
with a disgruntled meow. The cat swiped at her hand
with his sharp claws.

"All right, all right, I'm getting up."

The words were not enough to convince the tomcat.
Claire groaned as she sat up, much harder to do with
Urchin now crouched on her stomach.

And then it hit her. It was Saturday, the day of the
cupcake sale.

Claire jumped out of bed and hurried to feed the cat
before he mutilated her further. She treated the scratch
on her hand, combed her hair, and put it back in a clip.
Her stomach was doing somersaults with excitement

and nerves as she finished, looking herself in the eye in the mirror.

"You prepared for this. You can do this."

And she *had* prepared. Last night, they'd frosted two-hundred and forty of the cupcakes, the rest she had left unfrosted on purpose so she could do them fresh in the afternoon. She had bought special tiered racks to display them on, which she would put on top of the glass display case. She had Hailey and Maxi coming in to help her with the influx of extra customers she expected. She had cardboard boxes at the ready to put the baked goods in. She had done everything she could to promote the sale.

As she scooted to work in her Vespa, she thought about Rob. She felt guilty about the way she'd treated him, but it was too late to turn back now. Or was it?

The lights were already on at Bradford Breads. The shades were up, revealing the interior. Claire hesitated mere feet from her store, but curiosity overwhelmed her. Had he taken her advice and done something to the arrangement inside?

He would never know if she peeked. Checking the street—devoid of people or vehicles that early in the morning—Claire hurried over to the window. She cupped her hands and peered through the glass.

Rows upon rows of bread, buns, and bagels

awaited customers. They were stacked neatly on shelves taking up the bulk of the inside space, forming makeshift aisles with a clear path to the front counter and the register there. To the left was a table with yet more buns placed in baskets the way she'd wanted to do yesterday before she'd thought better of it. On the other side was a cozy little cluster of four tables arranged at an angle to one another with red napkin holders to match the color of the logo. Claire couldn't help but smile. He had taken her advice, after all.

Then her gaze caught movement. Rob had just come out of the back, presumably the kitchen, and had a loaf of bread in either hand. Her heart pounded at the prospect of being caught. She turned on her heel and fled across the street.

She felt ridiculous. Would he ever want to be business associates or friends after the way she'd treated him? She didn't have time to feel sorry for herself. Today was the big day, and she had work to do.

She worked quickly, pulling the cupcake containers out of the fridge, gingerly opening the tops, not wanting to disturb the frosting. She brought them out front and arranged them on the tiered displays. The pipes made an ominous clanking overhead. Claire winced but tried to ignore it. She had work to do. As long as the groaning of the pipes didn't scare off her customers, she would be fine.

What next? Maybe she should cut up part of the sandcastle cake today and give out pieces as free samples. She could cut from the back and leave the front as a display. She removed it from the glass case carefully, not disturbing any of the artfully arranged turrets. She placed it squarely in the middle of her cupcakes, two tiers on either side, and rounded the counter to see how they looked from the front.

Beautiful. She couldn't help but smile, an expression that shrank quickly as the pipes clanged again, the groaning increasing. That one sounded different than the other groans.

Claire tilted her head up and squinted.

There was a new rust stain on the tin ceiling, and…

Wait, were those drops of water?

Drip. Drip.

Claire followed their descent to the floor, where a small puddle had formed.

Oh no!

Pop. Pop. Pop. More leaks opened in the ceiling, bigger this time. And then…

Crash!

One section of the tin ceiling smashed to the floor, a

torrent of water behind it soaking the bakery floor, the tabletops, and the cupcakes on display.

"No!"

Everything was ruined. The pastries in the case, the cupcakes, the sandcastle cake, and Claire's dreams.

CHAPTER TWENTY-THREE

With twenty minutes left until Rob opened the doors of his newest bakery to the public, he paused and surveyed his shop. Bread lined every available surface, including the table he'd initially allotted for Claire. That table still knotted his stomach. All morning, he'd caught himself glancing across the street, hoping she would come over to tell him she changed her mind. He'd seen a shadow outside earlier, but no one was there, only a glimpse of her opening the side door leading to the kitchen in her bakery.

Unable to help himself, he stared across the street again. The cheery Sandcastles sign over the door looked the same as ever, but something wasn't right. He frowned. Where was Claire with her sandwich board promoting the sale? Why was her bakery still dark? And who was that hammering on her door? A familiar-looking petite blonde in a pencil skirt, cupping her hands around her eyes as she peered inside. Surely the town wasn't *that* eager for a cupcake sale.

Rob didn't like the feeling in his stomach. Wasn't that blonde one of Claire and Jane's friends? The one he met briefly when they searched for Addie?

It didn't matter that Claire might not welcome his presence—especially *this* morning. He needed to check it out. As he headed across the street, a second figure joined the first. This one, he recognized: Claire's assistant, Hailey. What were they looking at in the window?

"Is something wrong, ladies?"

Both of them jumped at the sound of his voice. Hailey turned, her face as white as a sheet. She pointed mutely at the window.

Frowning, Rob leaned forward and squinted through the sunlight reflecting off the glass. The interior of the shop was a disaster. Cupcakes were strewn everywhere. Frosting blobs marred the glass case. Part of the tin ceiling lay on the floor, an inch or more of water covering it. A slow drip rippled the water from overhead.

The bakery was in a sorry state, but…

"Where's Claire?"

The blonde, he couldn't recall her name, frowned and shook her head. "I don't know. I was supposed to meet her here this morning to help open for the sale. People will be arriving soon."

He turned to her assistant in the hopes of finding an answer. "Do you know where she is?"

The younger woman shook her head, looking every bit as distressed and lost.

He tried the front door—locked. Maybe Claire was around back. He rushed around to the side kitchen entrance, the two women trailing after him.

The kitchen wasn't in much better shape. Although the bulk of the water had hit the front of the store, enough had rained down here to cause a damp sheen over the tiles and ruin the frosting on the neatly arranged cupcakes on the table.

Claire sat on a stool, a cupcake in her hand. She looked over at them clustered in the doorway. "At least I was able to save a few."

She looked so forlorn that he wanted to take her in his arms, but he couldn't do that. "What happened?" he asked.

Claire unwrapped the cupcake and took a bite. "I should have listened to Ralph and replaced the pipes." The words were muffled because she'd shoved a big piece of cupcake in, but Rob understood.

The blonde pushed past him and rushed to Claire, hugging her. "What happened?"

"Pipes burst." Claire took another bite. "At least I found the main valve and shut it off. Sally would be proud."

"Are all the cupcakes ruined?" Hailey asked, making her way to the fridge.

"There are still several dozen in there, but the place is ruined, so I guess the sale is ruined." Claire's flat tone pinched Rob's heart. Suddenly, he had an idea. "The cupcake sale isn't ruined."

Claire looked up. She was still frowning, but a spark of hope flared in her eyes. "What do you mean? Of course it is. I can't open the shop. Most of the cupcakes are soaked."

He pointed at the containers in the fridge. "But not all of them. These are still perfect. There must be five or six dozen here."

She pressed her lips together and shook her head. "But the shop…"

The blonde turned, assessing Rob with curiosity. "What are you getting at?"

Rob met the blonde's gaze. "I'm not sure we were

introduced during the search for Jane's mother. I'm Rob." He stuck out his hand.

"I know." She smiled, placing her hand in his. "I'm Maxi."

He nodded, feeling a bit out of place. "Well, Maxi. Do you think you can take Claire home and return here in—" He checked his watch. "Fifteen minutes? I think she's going to want to change out of those wet clothes."

That stirred Claire to a bit of her normal luster. "What do you mean?"

"I mean you have a cupcake sale to run."

"Like I said, I don't have a store."

"No, but I do. We'll move all these containers and the tiered displays to my store."

"I couldn't."

He ignored her protests and carefully pulled the containers out of the fridge, piling them one atop another. "I already offered you a table in my store. You're going to use it. We'll put up a sign sending your customers across the street."

"You don't have to do this," Claire said in a small voice. But the color had returned to her cheeks and the spark to her eyes. "Your offer applied when I had a space to offer you as well. Cross-promotion, remember? Now I have nothing, and I don't want to take away from your sale."

He smiled at her, teasing a smile out of her in return. "But you forget. If we send all your customers to my store, I'll be benefitting too." He nodded to Maxi, spurring both women into action. "Come on. We have customers waiting."

She hesitated a moment before turning to follow her friend out of her store. Hailey had already grabbed the sandwich board and was making a sign.

At the door, Claire paused and turned to look at him. "Thank you."

He needed nothing else.

Hailey watched Rob Bradford as he gathered the cupcakes. This was the guy Claire had seen as the enemy? More like a knight in shining armor. He didn't have to help them out. He could have just stayed over in his bakery and let the disaster put them out of business. Hailey was sure their customers would have found their way across the street without a sign at Sandcastles.

"So, what's your plan?" Hailey asked.

"I'm going to set up some tables for the cupcakes, and you guys can sell from there. Does that sound good? If you have a better idea, I'm all ears."

Hailey appreciated that he wanted her input. "That's a great idea and very generous. I was wondering, though. Maybe we could bring some of the ingredients for more cupcakes. The cabinets didn't get wet, and the more we sell, the more money Claire can make toward fixing this." Hailey gestured toward the ceiling.

"Good point. Let's bring them."

Hailey started gathering ingredients. "I hope she won't be out of business for too long." *And I won't be without a paycheck for too long.*

"Oh, don't you worry. I can rearrange my store so she can sell from there." His brow creased with concern as he glanced at Hailey. "Naturally, I'll need extra help. I'll pay you to work the same hours you do here, maybe a little extra since you'll be helping the bread customers too."

Hailey liked the guy. He was perceptive and very sweet. He must really have a crush on Claire to go to all that trouble.

"We can make do with one storefront until Claire gets the pipes fixed. Unless Claire doesn't want to." Rob looked up from the cupcakes at Hailey. "Do you think she'll ever stop seeing me as the enemy?"

Hailey had a feeling she already had, but a little encouragement from Hailey couldn't hurt. "Maybe I can help with that." Hailey piled the baking ingredients she'd collected on top of the cupcake containers in Rob's arms. "Now let's get across the street. We have a lot of work to do if we are going to pull this sale off."

axi had called Jane on the way to Claire's cottage, and she showed up as Maxi was blow-drying Claire's hair. Claire sat in the vanity chair in her bedroom wrapped in a terry robe. Even though her shop had just been ruined, she actually didn't feel so bad.

Jane pulled open the closet. "Maybe you should wear something less—" Jane glanced down at Claire's wet clothing now on the floor. "Dowdy."

"My clothes aren't dowdy." Claire looked at the pile uncertainly.

"Well, it wouldn't hurt to put on something a little nicer than a gray T-shirt. I mean you will be waiting on half the town, and you want to make a nice impression."

Claire pushed Maxi away as she tried to curl her hair. "I think everyone in town knows me already." She didn't miss the look that Maxi and Jane exchanged in the mirror. She knew what they were up to. They were trying to make her look nice for Rob Bradford. Claire was much too mature for that sort of thing. Besides, she liked the way she looked already.

"I'm really sorry this happened," Jane pulled out a pretty pink short-sleeved shirt with turquoise trim around the neck and arms and laid it on the bed.

Claire's heart plummeted. Despite her hopeful feelings that Rob's generous offer might save the cupcake sale, the fact still remained that her shop was ruined. How could her business survive?

"Might be a blessing in disguise." Maxi placed a mascara wand and lipstick in front of Claire.

"How to you figure that?" Claire asked, ignoring the makeup in front of her.

"Insurance." Maxi opened the mascara and put it in Claire's hand.

"Insurance?" Claire started to apply automatically, curious about Maxi's statement.

"You have insurance for Sandcastles, right? Well, before this, you were going to fix the pipes on your dime, but now that the pipes have burst, you can put in a claim and let the insurance company pay for it."

"Good thinking. Get some use out of those high premiums you pay." Jane pulled out a pair of off-white linen capri's with thin turquoise stripes. "So, it turns out Rob really is a nice guy. I hate to say I told you so."

Jane's good-natured barb hit home. "I guess I was wrong about him. I feel terrible."

"Don't worry," Maxi said. "It's easy to misconstrue things when it involves things close to our hearts. Like my relationship with James."

Claire glanced up at her friend. She thought she'd sensed something wrong between them earlier but had been so wrapped up in her own problems she hadn't been paying attention. "Is something wrong?"

Maxi smiled. "No. Well, things are *different* since the kids left. But I misconstrued that as James losing interest in our marriage and in me. It turns out we just need to adjust."

"That makes sense. It's a big adjustment going from a houseful to nothing," Jane said.

"Yes, and I didn't have a lot to occupy my time, so I overanalyzed everything. I was too close to the situation. But everything is good now, and I'm even going to start drawing again. James suggested it, actually."

"That's wonderful," Jane said.

Claire agreed, even though she still saw a shadow of doubt in Maxi's eyes.

"I guess I've done the same thing with Mom," Jane said. "I couldn't look at it objectively because I'm too close to it."

"And now you can?" Claire asked.

Jane shrugged. "A little bit more. It's still gut-wrenching, but I think I know what the right decision is."

"I suppose that I have been blowing things out of proportion. Sandcastles is my baby, so it's hard not to get emotional. Maybe it really was a blessing that the pipes burst. I would have had to close the bakery to fix them anyway. I would have had to take out a loan to cover the repairs and backfill money lost from not being open with my savings. Maybe now I'll be able to keep my savings if insurance pays for it." Claire smiled at her two friends. "I'm sorry if I acted kind of crazy about Bradford Breads."

Maxi put her hand on Claire's shoulder. "No need to apologize. Sometimes you just have to take a step back from the situation."

"Speaking of which." Claire pushed back from the vanity and grabbed the outfit Jane had laid out. "We better get going. I have a cupcake sale to run."

CHAPTER TWENTY-FIVE

*C*laire had never seen so many people packed into one small shop. Despite the locals and tourists descending on the new bakery in droves, Rob had found the time to move the tables from in front of Claire's store and arrange them on the sidewalk in front of his. The interior of the store was dedicated not to sitting space but to cupcakes and bread.

The men and women stepping into the store were immediately drawn to the cupcakes, which now sat on freshly washed tiers. A sign in front of the table read "Sandcastles." The sign was a surprise. When in the world had Rob had time to make that?

Maxi stood next to the cash register, ringing up orders and recording every sale in a little notebook to

i

keep track of cupcake revenue. Jane had rushed back home but promised to bring Addie later on.

Claire's face hurt from smiling at everyone through endless explanations of why she wasn't across the street. The notice Hailey had put on the sandwich board had done its job of directing customers in here. Hailey was kept busy helping customers with both bread and cupcake purchases, and it appeared she and Rob had quickly formed a bond of some sort.

The bell over the door tinkled, as it did constantly throughout the day. It was approaching noon, and Claire would have been out of cupcakes soon, but she'd snuck into Rob's bakery kitchen and scrounged together a new batch. As soon as they cooled, she would send Hailey in to frost them and bring them out to sell.

Two old men entered the store, looking bewildered at the mass of people moving from shelf to shelf and plucking it clean of bread. They scanned the interior until they spotted her brightly colored table. Then, with matching smiles, Harry and Bert made their way over to her.

"Looks like we're almost too late!" Bert exclaimed.

"I have more cupcakes in the back," she assured them, her smile genuine. "The new flavors are going fast, though. You'd better grab some while you can."

Harry adjusted his glasses and leaned in. "What flavors do you have, now?"

Claire launched into the spiel she had memorized by this time. Lemon raspberry, chocolate mocha, cookies and cream, red velvet, and of course, the traditional chocolate and vanilla. Harry and Bert both asked for a box containing one of each. Claire obliged.

As she gently slipped the cupcakes into the rectangular boxes, she said, "I'm afraid your regular table isn't available this morning. I would have saved it for you if I could."

"Why is the store closed?" Bert asked.

Claire stifled a sigh. It was a question she'd fielded endlessly that morning. Fortunately, her back was turned, and they wouldn't see the slip in her smile. She took a deep breath, pasted it back on, and turned, offering them each their boxes.

"I had an incident at the store with the pipes. Until Ralph replaces them, I'll be closed. But Rob Bradford was kind enough to lend me this table so no one will miss out on the cupcake sale today."

"That's a stand-up guy," Bert replied with a nod.

Claire's gaze travelled to the swinging door leading to the kitchen. Rob walked out with a tray of bread to replenish the dwindling supplies on his shelves. In giving her the extra space to display her wares, he had moved much of his bread back to the kitchen.

He caught her watching and smiled. She couldn't help herself. She beamed back.

She had misjudged him. If Rob wanted to put her out of business, he would have left her in her kitchen, sobbing into her cupcakes. Instead, he had organized his space to save her cupcake sale and had motivated her out of her dour mood. If not for him, she would still be wallowing in misery, stuffing her face with cupcakes in the flooded bakery she owned.

Her problems weren't solved, but at least she had today.

"How long will the bakery be closed?" asked Harry, jarring Claire out of her thoughts.

She fought back a grimace. "I don't know for sure. Ralph told me two or three weeks initially, but I haven't booked him in yet. It's Saturday, so I'll have to call him on Monday unless he happens to stop by the sale."

"Two or three weeks! During summer?"

"I'm afraid so." To stem any further questions, she patted him on the arm and pointed toward the cash register, where Maxi perched on a stool. "You can pay for those over there, with Maxi. If you're also buying bread, you can pay for it at the same time. We're keeping track of what's what."

Reluctantly, the two men left, making room for more customers to step in. Claire handed out boxes and explained the flavors, smiling all the while until her cheeks hurt. Out of the corner of her eye, she noticed Maxi's husband, James, step into the store. He was a distinguished man with a well-trimmed beard and hair threaded through with silver. Even when he wore casual slacks and a polo shirt, like today, he somehow seemed as though he wore a suit. Claire followed him with her eyes as he made his way through the store to the front, sparing Claire no more than a glance and a nod in greeting.

For a second, Claire worried that James was unhappy that Maxi was helping with the sale, but the tension drained out of her as James reached his wife. They smiled at each other, and he leaned forward to kiss her cheek. Although they were too far away for Claire to hear what they were saying, he didn't seem angry. He seemed attentive, if the hand lingering lightly on her arm was any indication. She said something more to him then applied herself to helping the next customer in line. He didn't seem put off at the change in her attention.

Claire's gaze was drawn to the doorway, where an older man had just entered. He searched the crowd. His eyes lit, and a smile cracked his face as he found his target. "Rob!"

Claire watched Rob turn at the mention of his name. A look of surprise spread on his face. "Frank!"

The men strode toward each other, meeting in front of Claire. They hugged, genuinely happy to see each other.

"What's going on with you? Did you come all the way down for this?" Rob asked.

"Wouldn't miss it, my friend." Frank surveyed the store. "It's looking good. Little small." His gaze fell on Claire's sign. "Sandcastles. Isn't that the bakery across the street?"

"It is."

"Why aren't you open over there?" Frank stepped closer, squinting at the cupcakes in the tiered display.

"I had a problem with the pipes."

Frank nodded knowingly and glanced up at Rob. "Let me guess. My man Rob here took you in. Reminds me of old times."

"Old times?" Claire asked.

Frank stuck his hand out, and they shook. "Frank Martin. I owned the bakery across from Bradford Breads in Bar Harbor. Rob and I used to do a lot of cross-promotions. Made those last years before my retirement really profitable."

Bar Harbor? That was where Peter and Sandee had said Rob put the bakery out of business.

"You *retired* and closed your bakery on purpose?" Claire asked.

Frank shrugged and went back to inspecting her cupcakes. "Yeah, none of my kids wanted to run it, so I just shut down."

Peter and Sandee had been telling tales. Had they made it up or just assumed? It didn't really matter. They had been wrong about Rob. But then, Claire had already come to that conclusion on her own.

Frank picked up a chocolate cupcake. "I used to bake a mean cupcake myself, you know."

Rob laughed. "He sure did. Yours weren't as good as Claire's though."

"You don't say. I guess I'll have to try some." Frank picked out three cupcakes while continuing to talk to Rob. "I'm down for a few days. Maybe we could get together."

"Sounds great."

Frank nodded and handed his three cupcakes to Claire, who put them in a box. "Well, I know you're busy. Give me a shout tonight, and we'll catch up."

He sauntered off to the cash registers, but Rob remained at Claire's side.

"He's a nice guy. Baked a great apple pie."

"He's not the only nice guy." Claire tilted her head to meet Rob's smiling eyes. Out of the corner of her eye, she caught Sally at the wheat bread giving her a knowing look. She tried not to feel too uncomfortably aware of the man standing next to her. They were adults, after all. Business owners. Colleagues of sorts. And she *was* in his store.

"How is the sale going?" he asked.

"Wonderfully. I think I might need to use your kitchen again if the customers keep up through the afternoon. What time do you usually close?"

"Five o'clock on weekends, but we can stay open later if there's still a steady stream of customers."

We?

"You should take a break and find yourself something to eat. Maxi or Hailey can cover for you while you do."

Claire smiled. "You're always thinking of others, aren't you? What about taking a break yourself?"

"I had a sandwich in the kitchen, but I could be persuaded." He trailed off as the door opened with a jingle of bells. When he smiled widely at the newcomers, Claire turned to see who had arrived. Jane stood next to her mother, cradling Addie's arm and taking some of her weight as she moved. The old woman tried to shake off her daughter, but her foot must still hurt because the attempt was half-hearted. The pair carefully made their way over to Claire and Rob.

"Addie, it's so good to see you," Claire exclaimed.

The old woman blinked owlishly. "You too."

The terse answer and her blank look told Claire that today wasn't as good as she had hoped. She met Jane's helpless gaze.

"I'm glad you're here. Should I box up some cupcakes for you and Addie?"

Jane nodded. "Thank you. We're here to pick up a couple loaves of bread too."

Rob gestured at the shelves. "Be my guest. I'm happy to talk about a more regular delivery at a later date."

Jane nodded but didn't commit. "I guess we'd better move along. You're busy, and Mom can't stay on her feet too long." She leaned in and whispered to Claire, "The outfit looks great."

Claire self-consciously straightened the black apron she'd put over the pink-and-turquoise top and quickly boxed up the cupcakes for her friend, the last of the new flavors. As she turned back, she saw Addie lean closer to Rob with a wink.

"Don't forget our date."

Rob gave her a chagrined smile as Jane led the old woman away. The moment they were out of earshot, the babble swallowing up any sound Claire would make, she asked. "Date?"

Rob smiled. "I believe she thinks I'm taking her to a high school dance."

"Ah." It worried Claire that Addie's memory was so muddled, but at least she seemed happy.

"Speaking of dates," Rob said, leaning closer as he lowered his voice. "Maybe we should have dinner together sometime soon. We can talk about how we can work together to promote our bakeries and how to keep yours in business during the repairs."

Did he say *dates*? As in like a business date or…? Claire's heart fluttered in her throat. She swallowed before she answered in a small voice, "Why? I've been such a jerk to you for no reason at all. You've been nothing but kind this whole time, but I just couldn't see it. For what it's worth, I'm sorry for the way I acted. I really—" She swallowed again, and her gaze dropped to her hands, which she twisted nervously. "I really appreciate what you've done here for me today."

Rob reached out to put his hand over hers, stilling her nervous movement. His hand was warm, as were his eyes when she looked up again. "It's my pleasure. I meant it when I said I want us to work together. I'm sure we can find a way to benefit both our businesses. Besides, we can't let Hailey go without work while

Sandcastles is being repaired. She's a great worker, and I've seen what she drives. She needs the money."

"That would be nice, but I'm not sure we'd have much to talk about. You could keep Hailey on, but I don't have a shop to work out of at the moment, and I don't know for sure when I'll reopen."

"This arrangement seems to be working," Rob said, gesturing to the table. "You didn't have trouble working in my kitchen either."

Claire frowned. "What are you saying?"

His eyes twinkled. "I'm saying you can set up here until your shop is up and running."

Claire resisted the urge to pinch herself and check if she was dreaming. "You would do that for me? You don't even know me."

He squeezed her hand. "Not yet, but I plan to."

CHAPTER TWENTY-SIX

*C*laire would have been hard-pressed to believe it at the time, but now, three weeks later, she could see that the pipes bursting in Sandcastles had a silver lining. It had opened her up to trusting Rob. That became a cornerstone of their working relationship.

Since then, Claire had worked from a small corner of Bradford Breads. Her profits were carefully listed in a ledger next to the cash register, and every Friday, Rob paid her promptly for the sales she'd made. Her regulars griped about not having their usual tables to eat breakfast at, especially if the weather outside was too dreary or blustery to sit out at the sidewalk tables. Very soon, they would have nothing to complain about.

The best part was that insurance had paid for most

of the repairs. Claire didn't have to take out a loan, and the dent in her savings wasn't too bad either.

She'd hired Ralph that same day to begin work on the pipes. He was giving them a complete overhaul. She suspected he was giving her a break on the price. Supplying him with cookies, brownies, and cupcakes every day might have had something to do with that.

It was busy having both of them in the bread shop, but Hailey kept things running smoothly. Rob had insisted on paying her extra because it was more work. Claire didn't argue. She knew Hailey was worth every penny.

They operated surprisingly well together, too, she mused as they strolled along the Marginal Way, a habit they'd formed while speaking of business. He loved the calming effect of the ocean every bit as much as she did. It felt less formal than dinner together—which they'd also shared several times—but the fact that they were coming up there to brainstorm joint marketing strategies for her bakery reopening in another week made the well-worn path something indefinable. Their talks were starting to feel less like business and more like dates, especially when they veered to more personal matters.

Claire still hadn't confessed to Rob that she *had* been the girl he kissed so many years ago. She hadn't worked up the courage. But sometimes, as they walked on the narrow path, their hands brushed, and she wondered, *What if...?*

"You know the last thing I want is to take business away from you." Rob sounded hesitant, which jarred her back to the conversation at hand: an idea she had to integrate their two bakeries a little more.

"I know. That's why we would exchange goods." She paused at the bottom of the cliffside path. The wind whipped her hair in front of her eyes. She tucked it behind her ear instead and craned her neck back to look him in the eye. "I think it's a good idea. I would make sweet breads like banana bread, chocolate zucchini bread, that sort of thing. In exchange, you give me loaves of your bread to use for sandwiches in my shop. I noticed you don't offer drinks in yours, only bread, so customers are more likely to stay and have a meal in mine. If we put stickers on the bags saying those things come from each other's shops, I'm sure we'll find curious customers who travel across the road for more."

"You already make bread," he pointed out, his face expressionless.

"And I hate it," she confessed. "I've never done a good job at it, and for the amount of work it takes, I'd rather bake a batch of croissants. I could use the bakery case space for pastries. Besides, I've tasted your bread. It's much better than mine ever was."

Was it her imagination, or was that a blush creeping up Rob's neck?

"My daughter suggested the idea," she added. "She says it will be good for marketing to have each other's products so integrated in our shops."

One side of his mouth lifted in a smirk. "I'd like to meet Tammi someday. She sounds like she has a good head on her shoulders."

Claire beamed. "She does. She's very smart. Takes after her mother."

"Then I very much look forward to meeting her." Rob spoke the words with a distracted air as he approached one of the large cedar trees dotting the path. Without warning, he took Claire's hand in his and tugged her along after him, into a secluded area off the path next to the tree.

It was the same place he had kissed her when she was a teenager. Claire's stomach swirled with butterflies. She bit her lower lip, uncertain.

His eyes were warm on her face. "Do you remember this place?"

"Of course. I've lived here my whole life."

"Well, I haven't, but I remember it very well." He

tucked a strand of her hair behind her ear. "I once kissed a very special girl in this spot."

The butterflies swelled until they felt like songbirds. "I know," Claire confessed.

One of Rob's eyebrows quirked up. "Oh, so you remember now." It was statement more than question.

"I never forgot."

He squeezed her hand. "I never forgot either. It's partly why I came back to Lobster Bay, hoping to find you again."

Claire didn't know what to say. She was afraid to breathe and ruin the moment.

"But you know, there is something I regret about that night."

Claire stiffened. "What is that?"

"That I didn't do this a second time." He leaned down and kissed her.

❀

Maxi strolled along the Marginal Way with Jane. There were only a few people on the path ahead. A group of teenagers, a family with a baby in a stroller, and a curvy woman and tall man. Did she recognize those two people?

"I think I'm going to do it," Jane announced.

Maxi glanced sideways at her friend. "Do what?"

"Put my mom in a memory care facility. I've had time to visit a few now, and there's one a couple of miles away that seems like just the fit for her. All I have to do is find a way to break it to her and hope she doesn't hate me for it." She paused, wrapping her arms around her middle. "Of course, she'll forget as soon as I tell her, so at least there's that."

"You have to think about what's right for both of you. It isn't fair to you to be her caretaker, and it isn't fair to her to have a caretaker who has her attention elsewhere half the time. Your mom might need to adjust, but I'm sure she'll be better off this way. What did your sister think?"

Jane bit her lip and tucked her hair behind her ear. "I haven't told her yet."

Maxi faltered, almost tripping over a rock. "What? Don't you think you should?"

Jane sighed. "I suppose I'll have to. Not that she'll care one way or another."

Maxi remembered how hard it had been for Jane when Andrea had left town. Jane had idolized her older sister. "You should give Andie a chance. I know you two are estranged, but this could bring you together. I'm sure she cares."

Jane pressed her lips together. Maxi could see the

urge to contradict her welling up behind Jane's closed-off expression, but her friend hated confrontation. She swallowed the protest. When she laid a hand on top of Maxi's arm, stopping her, Maxi assumed it was to change the subject.

Fine. Maxi could take a hint.

"Isn't that Claire and Rob?" Jane's eyes almost bugged out of her head.

Maxi followed her gaze to the figures up ahead. They had caught up a bit because the pair had stepped off the path and were under the base of a big cedar tree. The man, almost certainly Rob, was kissing the woman, definitely Claire.

Maxi grinned. "It looks like they're finally getting along."

Jane snorted and elbowed Maxi in the side. "Maybe we should give them their privacy."

"Only if we're allowed to tease her about this afterward."

Jane laughed and linked her arm through Maxi's, steering her around to walk back the way they came. Maxi couldn't believe she saw Claire kissing someone, maybe even for the first time since her divorce. The two bakers were perfect together. She and Jane had seen it from the beginning. Everyone should have someone to take comfort in.

Like James? The warm feeling dimmed a bit as she and Jane walked back toward the beach. She and James weren't what they had once been, but Maxi was taking steps to enliven their marriage. She didn't want it to turn stale and resentful. She was making good progress on that front. At least she *thought* she was.

"If you're going to put Addie in a facility, what will happen to Tides?" Maxi asked.

"I'll still run it, I suppose. It's a family legacy. I sort of promised Mom I would."

"Are you sure that's what you want?"

Jane hesitated for a moment too long, giving away her misgivings. "I'd rather not, but there's no one else. The fate of Tides is entirely on my shoulders."

Maxi squeezed her friend, offering what support she could. "As long as you remember you don't have to be in this alone. If you need us, you will always have me and Claire, even if she has a boyfriend now."

They both laughed, lightening the mood. Maxi resisted looking over her shoulder to spy on the couple in question. Their lives might be changing, but that didn't mean it was a bad thing.

Maybe it was a chance for a new beginning for all of them.

****

If you liked this book, then you'll be happy to know that the adventures Lobster Bay aren't over. Are you wondering if Jane is really making the right decision or if her sister will come back and help her out? What about Maxi… is James really finally ready to let her realize her artistic dreams, or is he just trying to "keep her busy" so she doesn't find out what he's really up to?

Find out as the adventures in Lobster Bay continue:

Changing Tides (book 2)

Join my newsletter for sneak peeks of my latest books and release day notifications:

https://lobsterbay1.gr8.com

Follow me on Facebook:

https://www.facebook.com/meredithsummers

ALSO BY MEREDITH SUMMERS

Lobster Bay Series:

Saving Sandcastles (Book 1)

Changing Tides (book 2)

Making Waves (Book 3)

ABOUT THE AUTHOR

Meredith Summers writes cozy mysteries as USA Today Bestselling author Leighann Dobbs and crime fiction as L. A. Dobbs.

She spent her childhood summers in Ogunquit Maine and never forgot the soft soothing feeling of the beach. She hopes to share that feeling with you through her books which are all light, feel-good reads.

Join her newsletter for sneak peeks of the latest books and release day notifications:

https://lobsterbay1.gr8.com

This is a work of fiction.

None of it is real. All names, places, and events are products of the author's imagination. Any resemblance to real names, places, or events are purely coincidental, and should not be construed as being real.

SAVING SANDCASTLES

Copyright © 2020

Meredith Summers

http://www.meredithsummers.com

All Rights Reserved.

No part of this work may be used or reproduced in any manner, except as allowable under "fair use," without the express written permission of the author.

Made in the USA
Monee, IL
01 March 2021

61689498R00154